COSEGA SHIFT

Book Three of the Cosega Sequence

BRANDT LEGG

LAUGHING RAIN

Cosega Shift (Book Three of the Cosega Sequence)

Published in the United States of America by Laughing Rain

Cataloging-in-Publication data for this book is available from the Library of Congress.
ISBN-13: 978-1-935070-09-2
ISBN-10: 1-935070-09-6

Cover designed by: Eleni Karoumpali

PUBLISHER'S NOTE

This book is a work of fiction. Names, characters, places and incidents are products of the author's imagination or are used fictitiously. Any resemblance to actual persons, living or dead, businesses, events or locales is entirely coincidental.

BrandtLegg.com

This book is dedicated to Teakki and Ro

1

Friday July 21st

The shot rang deafeningly loud. An explosion of blood and flesh covered his chest and face. Rip's last thought before he collapsed into the water was of the Eysen, and the incomplete Cosega Sequence.

He flailed in the shallow water, coming up in a pool of blood. Suddenly, rough hands were on him, pulling his shirt, dragging him, and dropping him on the dusty shore. He rolled over and saw a shotgun pointed at his face, then looked into the eyes of the man who'd been dogging him every step since he'd found the Eysen.

"I was beginning to think you might not really exist Gaines."

Rip realized he hadn't been hit. The blood and guts, now mostly washed off his body, were Leary's, who lay dead a few feet away.

"In case you haven't guessed, I'm Special Agent Dixon Barbeau with the Federal Bureau of Investigation."

Rip nodded and sighed, happy to be alive, and almost relieved it was finally finished.

"For the world's most wanted man, there wasn't one reliable sighting of you until now," Barbeau said. "Where's the girl?"

"I've got nothing to say," Rip said. "Aren't you going to read me my rights?"

"You know professor, there's a lot I don't understand about this case, but one thing I do know for sure is that if I arrest you, it's the same as if I'd let Leary over there kill you . . . you'll be dead before the end of the day."

Rip looked at Barbeau, confused.

"I'm not saying I won't still be after you, I'm just saying today isn't the day I arrest you," Barbeau said frowning.

"You're letting me go?"

"First, I need to know more about what's really happening."

"You're *letting* me *go?*" Rip repeated, looking around.

"This case isn't about a self-important, paranoid, half-crazy archaeologist stealing an artifact from a National Forest."

"I know. I'm glad you understand that much at least."

"Yeah, well, if I'm going to find out the truth, I need you alive. And, as I said, it's too dangerous to arrest you."

"How are you going to explain him?" Rip asked, pointing at Leary.

Barbeau glanced at the body with a disgusted look. "That bastard killed my partner. The scumbag is just paperwork now. There'll be an inquiry, which may take me away for a day, allowing you to get a lead. You did okay with that much of a head start last time, but don't blow it. And try not to get yourself killed. I've got another Vatican agent in custody, but more will be coming, and the NSA is your worst nightmare."

Rip stared at Barbeau, slowly getting to his feet. "But you're letting me go?"

Barbeau nodded.

"Thanks . . . or whatever," Rip said, looking for a long time into Barbeau's eyes before starting to run toward the plane. Hopefully, his dad's friend, Dyce, would still be there.

"Hey, Gaines!" Barbeau called.

"Yeah?" Rip stopped and turned back, thinking Barbeau had changed his mind.

"Is that Eysen really worth all this?" He waved his gun towards Leary and Hall, the motion implying a dozen other deaths, or at least Rip took it that way.

Rip looked directly at Barbeau. "It's worth the whole world."

2

Jaeger, the senior NSA official, watched the large screen in a darkened room about two hours south of Rip's location. The NSA command center in Phoenix, Arizona, like most of their operations, was highly classified. Two other operatives were seated at the large table.

"Barbeau let Gaines go," Jaeger said.

"Are you surprised?" an operative asked.

"Pleasantly." Jaeger almost smiled. "However, I've got less than three minutes to either have our people apprehend him, or let him board that plane."

Jaeger drummed his fingers on the table while viewing live footage of Gaines making his way to the landing strip. It wasn't as if the NSA didn't have significant reach outside the U.S., and they were particularly well represented in Mexico, Rip's likely destination, but each hour Gaines remained free made the situation harder to control. The person troubling him wasn't even Gaines. It was Booker Lipton. The report he'd just read on the President's summit, where all the players seeking Gaines were in attendance, confirmed that Booker wasn't playing ball.

Jaeger believed he had the FBI and White House under control, and the Vatican worried him only a little, especially with one of the Vatican's two lead agents dead and the other agent in custody. But Booker knew how to evade the NSA better than anyone, mainly because his companies were the primary manufacturers and suppliers of most of the monitoring equipment and software used by the intelligence community, including the NSA.

It made Jaeger nervous that many of Booker's ex-employees were now on the NSA staff. Others had trained large numbers of operatives on equipment use, and countless former NSA, CIA, FBI, DIA, and DHS agents were working for Booker's companies. "*Too damned incestuous,*" Jaeger had told his superiors more than once. If they let Gaines fly away on that plane, it would be increasingly difficult to prevent Booker from getting to him first.

The NSA had people who could attempt to understand the Eysen, but it was no ordinary computer, and it required more than technical know-how. Data intercepted from the Vatican made it clear that only Gaines could unlock its secrets. The NSA profile on the famed archaeologist made it abundantly clear that he would not help them. All along, Jaeger had worked to change that by having Gaines cooperate, unknowingly.

"We have to let him go . . . again," Jaeger said, pulling his drumming fingers into a fist and knocking twice on the table as the screen showed an image of Gaines nearing the plane.

"What about taking Booker into custody?" the operative asked.

"I considered it when we had him at the White House, but he'd be out in hours."

"What if we eliminated him?"

"That plan is already in place, should the need arise," Jaeger said.

"No easy task with his private army of spies, mercenaries, and trained agents."

"Far from guaranteed. And, let us not forget, Booker's plans may include the same for us."

Jaeger turned his attention to another screen and watched news coverage of Gaines' death. "Famed archaeologist, Ripley

Gaines, was killed today in a shootout with federal law enforcement. The bizarre case began ten days ago in Virginia with the professor's disappearance. He allegedly stole important artifacts that had been unearthed in the Jefferson National Forest. Gaines was subsequently charged with the murder of a lab worker, but those charges were later dropped. Viewers, please use discretion. The following footage contains graphic images of violence which some may find disturbing."

He mouthed the words as the anchor said them. Jaeger had written the copy two days earlier. The footage had been prepared by the same NSA lab that did the film of Gaines viewing photos of Josh Stadler's body and paying off the killers. Those images that Jaeger had shown to Sean Stadler on the way to Asheville.

"It's amazing. People go to the movies and watch Superman fly, dinosaurs eat people, and all kinds of murder and death, as realistic as if it happened in front of their eyes, and yet they never question what they see on the TV news," Jaeger said.

One of the others laughed. "TV news is an oxymoron."

Jaeger nodded, smiling, then flipped a switch. A previously dark monitor came to life, showing a live feed of a sleepy motel outside Flagstaff, Arizona. Agents were already there, waiting for Gale to make a move.

"Gaines ditched his tracking device, but apparently neglected to tell his girlfriend," Jaeger said. "Or she's playing it smart."

"Has she called Senator Monroe?" an operative asked.

"Not yet. Gale Asher has only made one phone call . . . to the last person you'd expect."

3

Booker stood holding a customized Kreighoff K80 shotgun as the clay pigeon zoomed far above his head. Skeet shooting helped him release anger, but he'd already said "pull" three times and had yet to fire a shot.

He knew the news reports of Rip's death were false, but for all practical purposes he might as well be dead. Booker had learned too late that the NSA had used his planned extraction site to undermine his relationship with Rip. The NSA operatives masquerading as FBI agents finalized the increasing mistrust between the two old friends. Rip might not give him another chance, and Booker had already used the Larsen surprise, his best hope.

"Pull," he repeated. This time he shot, blowing the target to dust.

The NSA had many advantages. They "owned" the President, and Attorney General, therefore the FBI. And, for the moment, they knew where Rip was and he did not. Booker's best guess was that Rip's father was helping him get into Mexico. The NSA had neutralized the FBI and would allow him to "escape", then watch every move. Booker and the NSA were locked in a chess match, with the winner taking the Eysen and all of its promised power.

There was one remaining bright spot. If all went well, Booker might soon have a very surprising new asset in the game.

"Pull!" Another disc was obliterated.

He got off three more perfect shots before his scrambled satphone buzzed. Booker looked up to the stratosphere, as if trying to spot the spy satellites that he knew were up there. Then, he answered the phone.

"Gale, thank you for putting up with all these annoying nuisances."

"I understand the precautions," she responded. Gale had called ninety minutes earlier, but not on a direct number, and it took a while to get the call transferred through channels. After that, arrangements needed to be made for a secure line.

"It's not easy to make an unmonitored call when the NSA is watching your every move," Booker said. "Wherever you are at the moment, they are there also."

"Rip is dead. Why would I still be under surveillance?"

Booker had anticipated this part of the conversation and debated the best way to play it. On one hand, he could deliver the good news, which she would eventually learn anyway. However, in spite of Larsen's assurances to the contrary, she was likely assisting the Vatican and/or the NSA. Gale's connection to his two competitors through her former lover and current friend, Senator Monroe, was too coincidental not to be an indication of a conspiracy. And if she knew that Rip was alive, Gale might not have a reason to continue communications with Booker.

"It's a complex and messy business, and there are many moving parts to all of this. Your relationships with Rip, Larsen, and Senator Monroe make you a person of interest, to say the least."

"You're a hypocrite!" Gale blasted. "You turned Rip against me because my friendship with Monroe scares you. What about *your* relationship with Monroe? If we were to judge people solely by the company they keep, you'd be in prison!"

"I don't hide my relationships from those closest to me," Booker countered.

"We were running for our lives. Rip didn't want me along, and I wasn't about to give him another reason not to take me."

"Just what is your interest in all this?" Booker asked, trying to avoid making her angrier.

"I'm the reporter. I get to ask the questions."

"Gale, you aren't ever going to write this story," Booker said calmly. "Maybe you should stop looking for the facts and start searching for the truth."

"Facts and truth aren't mutually exclusive."

"More often than not, they are."

"I didn't call you to debate philosophy. I need your help."

"I'm glad you contacted me, but I'm also curious. Why aren't you talking to Senator Monroe instead?"

"Because the Senator is in more trouble than I am."

4

Rip had a clear view of the plane and, more importantly, the pilot. It was definitely his dad's buddy, Dyce. No one else seemed to be there. He looked over his shoulder for the hundredth time – no sign of Barbeau or anyone else – and darted toward the plane.

"Rip!" Dyce shouted as he approached. "Damn, I was 'bout ready to give up on you son. Then I heard shots, figured you were close, or dead. Just decided to give you three more minutes, then planned on hightailing it outta here. Didn't want to get the plane, or myself, shot up. Are you okay?"

"Where's my dad?"

"They're watching him too close. He didn't want to risk it."

"Who?"

"Beats me. Don't you know?"

"Is he okay?"

"Was when I saw him last."

"Let's get out of here."

As they were strapping into the four-seater, Dyce's cell phone beeped. "Damn, it's your dad. Said he wouldn't call unless there was trouble," Dyce said, looking worried.

"Answer it."

"Yeah," Dyce said into the phone. "Then he looks pretty good for a dead man. Yeah, I'm sure. He's sitting right here if you want to talk to him."

Dyce handed Rip the phone and then started the engine.

"Dad?"

"Rip, the news is running a story that you were killed in a shootout with the feds."

"That's probably what they were planning, but I'm fine."

"Then I just blew your cover. They probably know where you are now. Sorry. I never would have called if—"

"Don't worry about it. We're moving. I'm disconnecting."

"God speed, Rip."

Seconds later, they were airborne. Jaeger saw it happen live on his big screen and hoped he had made the right decision. Barbeau watched from the ground, hoping the same thing.

Rip took the battery out of Dyce's phone, unaware that the NSA already knew his exact location. The plane's model number, fuel capacity, range, and numerous other factors were fed into an NSA computer that calculated potential flight paths and destinations. The results automatically updated each time the pilot made a turn. Jaeger already had teams scrambling in Mexico.

Barbeau waited twenty-five minutes before calling in. He would have liked to give Gaines more time to get away, but with an agent killed, he couldn't afford the risk. Already the details would need to be fudged, and an entire story created since Nanski would be a material witness. Nanski, apprehended and locked in the car since before Hall or Leary were killed, could testify as to times of shots and the plane taking off. Normally, it would be Barbeau's word against his, but eventually Nanski would be talking to the Attorney General, who would most likely side with the Vatican agent.

Without thinking, Barbeau pulled the folded evidence bag

from his pocket containing the dirt from Chimayó. Kneeling over Hall's body, he sprinkled the contents on his dead colleague. Then, the hardened FBI agent stared, anticipating something to happen, but knowing the sacred soil was powerless against a force as great as death. A simple lead bullet had stolen another life.

"How hard a life is to live and so easy to end," Barbeau whispered.

His sense of loss and grief took him by surprise. He didn't even think he liked Hall, but realized he had. Hall was like Barbeau, both dedicated agents working way beyond what was required. But, somehow, Hall had done it right, and managed some semblance of a life outside the Bureau.

Barbeau hadn't been envious of that. He respected it, admired Hall for it. He'd have to call Hall's girlfriend and tell her the god damned awful news. He'd say something nice that she wouldn't hear, but would always remember.

Barbeau looked over at Leary's bloody body, wishing he could resurrect the bastard just so he could punch his face a few times before shooting him all over again. He reached for invisible cigarettes, long ago given up, or was it for a flask. Damn, it wasn't there anymore either.

5

They landed on a remote runway, far better than the one they had lifted off from in Arizona. Dyce explained that American tourists flying their own planes to Mexico for vacations had once used the strip, but in recent years drug smugglers had taken it over and made improvements.

A driver waited, smoking a cigarette. Rip noticed a pile of butts by the car. "You're late," the old Mexican said in perfect English.

"I'll double your pay if you stop complaining now," Dyce said.

"Shoooot, you don't have enough to pay me half of what I'm worth. Probably expecting me to buy dinner too." The driver laughed.

He reminded Rip of Grinley, the old drug dealer who had helped them escape in Taos. For a moment, Rip thought of asking the driver if he knew him.

"Rip," Dyce began. "This is Elpate the Great, a very old and trusted friend."

"How did you get a name like that?" Rip asked while they drove a 1980s Honda Accord into the setting sun.

Elpate laughed. "I got it the old-fashioned way . . . I earned it."

"Elpate was a kingpin," Dyce explained.

"I don't recall. It was so long ago. Half the drugs they deal these days hadn't even been invented yet."

"Elpate isn't being modest. His brain cells are all fried," Dyce said. "But it's a good story. He started dealing pot and coke as a teenager, got smart *and* lucky. By age twenty-two he had conquered the known world, like Alexander the Great."

"Known world?"

"He controlled most of the coke and weed coming from Mexico into the U.S."

"Wow. Then how come he's driving this old junker?" Rip asked.

"Hey, man. Don't disrespect my wheels! You want to walk, gringo?"

"Sorry, I-I . . ." Rip stuttered.

"He's messing with you Rip," Dyce said. "He knows the car sucks. Elpate used to have two Porsches, a Ferrari, a Lamborghini, and a Rolls."

"I wish I could remember the Ferrari," Elpate said.

"Then he got busted," Dyce said. "DEA took it all. Gave him a couple of life sentences."

"Why aren't you still in jail?"

"You writing a book?" Elpate shot back.

"No, I—"

"Rip, he's messing with you again."

Elpate laughed. "I'm a reformed man."

"His attorneys got him off on appeal. Found some legal technicality," Dyce corrected.

"That's lucky," Rip said.

"Shooot. That may seem lucky to you, but I didn't get the Ferrari back."

Dyce and Elpate continued to rib each other. Rip, used to being exhausted, could barely keep his eyes open any longer. "You're safe now," Dyce told him. "Stretch out back there and get some rest. It'll be hours until we get there. I'll wake you."

Rip trusted Dyce, and did find some relief in finally being out of the U.S. and back on the ground. But he didn't feel *safe*, and wasn't sure he ever would again.

"I'll be okay," Rip said, rolling down his window as the driver and Dyce passed a joint between them. "Hey Dyce, you know my dad is 'Mr. Right Wing,' one of the most conservative talk radio hosts on the air?"

"Yeah, so?" he said, coughing out a cloud of smoke.

"How on earth did you two remain friends all these years?"

"Oh, well, remember that your dad and I were just kids when we met, and we stayed best friends all through school. That's too much history. Those friendships from youth, when the world seems so big, they never go away. There's just too much truth in them."

Rip wished he could have known his dad before politics and ideology ate his brain. They had never agreed on much, and Clastier drove a further wedge. Prior to his mother's death, she had wanted Rip to know about being a descendent of the church builders and to be allowed to study Clastier, but his father was adamantly opposed, saying it was all "fairytales and blather." The older Gaines wasn't Catholic, but did regularly attend church, although Rip wasn't sure which denomination – Methodist or Baptist. He always confused them. It was unclear to Rip just how much his father knew about Clastier, since they'd never discussed the subject.

His late uncle and Topper had introduced Rip to Clastier, at his mother's secret dying wish. At fifteen, Rip was already taking college courses and exploring numerous career paths. Neuroscience, astrophysics, and marine biology were among his many interests, but he was unable to choose one until he read Clastier's work. He learned quickly the "power of the papers", and why Clastier's writings had inspired an entire nineteenth century mountain town to construct a "church" to study them. Where those before him had sought the hidden meaning between the lines, Rip built his life around the mission of finding the hidden "impossible object" the Divinations promised. The words, *"Within the stone is a light, which will cause the holy city to collapse, for it shall erase the past, demonstrate all knowledge to be false and the scriptures to be a hoax,"* burned in him and focused, for the first time, his wild, insatiable mind.

Now here he was, driving into the night through the Mexican countryside with a couple of aging stoners. The engine of the 1980s Honda occasionally coughed and regularly wheezed, but the miles between Rip and all the troubles back in the States were adding up. At great cost he had the prize, and finally the exciting work of understanding just what that meant could truly begin. He needed to decode the Cosega Sequence in order to find out exactly what the Eysen was, who had built it, and, more importantly, why.

6

Booker typed Gale's location into an encrypted text and sent it to Kruse. He had anticipated her next request and sent another one to Larsen. "Stay put. I'll get someone to you in the next thirty minutes."

"I'm not going with anyone other than Larsen."

"He'll be there too. But Gale, I don't think you realize just how much danger you're facing."

"You're wrong about that. If I didn't know the situation, I would never have called you," Gale said bitterly. "Especially after you've made matters so much worse. I don't think *you* understand the situation."

"Then I look forward to our enlightening each other," Booker said. He'd been happy to end the call without having to tell her Gaines was actually alive. That task would fall to Larsen as soon as they were safely at their destination. Getting her there would be the trick. BLAX, the most elite unit of Booker's security squad, had two advantages over the NSA operatives watching her: surprise, and numbers.

Fortunately, Booker had been prepared for the extraction of Gale and Rip for days, and it had all come down to Flagstaff. The timing worked in Booker's favor as the NSA had only two operatives there. Twenty-three minutes after Booker and Gale spoke, an army of BLAX agents arrived. Although the NSA could also monitor the motel from satellites, that only helped against normal targets.

BLAX agents identified two vehicles, each containing two adult occupants. Only one was NSA, but they couldn't waste time determining which car. Gale left her room at the prearranged time and headed for the highway, quickly crossing the empty lanes. She walked casually along the shoulder, south toward Flagstaff, with her arm and thumb extended.

At the same time, BLAX agents implemented a "sun-pulse-shadow" to blanket a thousand-foot radius, effectively blocking all cell, Internet, and most importantly, satellite communications. One of Booker's companies had developed the technology, which had been sold exclusively to U.S. intelligence agencies. Also referred to simply as "the Haze" or "SPS," the equipment effectively made the NSA blind and deaf to the area. The Haze could be defeated, but only after a frustrating game of cat and mouse that could last hours.

The moment Gale left her room the NSA operatives had tried to contact Jaeger in the command center, but were blocked by the Haze. They pulled out of their parking space, but before they could reach the highway, all four tires were simultaneously shot out with silencer-equipped rifles. The NSA operatives, with weapons drawn, fled their car and headed to the highway, seeking cover along the way.

Kruse, Harmer, and Larsen picked up Gale in a rented van while another van, filled with BLAX agents, pulled into the motel lot directly in front of the NSA agents. They knew the NSA operatives would find a way to follow Gale, and therefore needed to be engaged. However, Booker was anxious to avoid killing U.S. agents, so BLAX used tranquilizers. It took less than ninety seconds to neutralize the NSA team and transfer them into the van. Later, they would be left in the desert, twenty minutes outside of town, just prior to when the drug would subside.

A dangerous side effect to using SPS was that the Haze left an electronic footprint that would signal Jaeger that Gale was gone and, more unfortunately, that Booker had her. Booker knew the risks, but he had to cripple the NSA's surveillance apparatus if he hoped to get her away safely. Still, it presented numerous problems, and he expected to hear from the Attorney General, or even the President.

Soon Gale, Larsen, Kruse, and Harmer were airborne, picked up in one of Booker's custom $22 million Augusta Westland AW101 VVIP helicopters. Flying at 180 miles per hour, they would be in Gale's chosen destination in about two hours. Booker would arrive to meet with them, but hadn't been planning on the trip, so he'd be four hours behind them. It was the last place in the world he wanted to go, but Gale would cooperate only if she could return to Taos.

Larsen sat across from Gale in one of the plush leather seats. Kruse and Harmer were a few rows back, reviewing the many possible locations where Rip might be.

"Do you know this is the same type of helicopter the President of the United States flies in, Marine One?" Larsen asked Gale. "But I think that this one must be nicer."

Gale stared blankly at him. "I don't give a damn about the President's helicopter *or* how many planes Booker has."

"Fine, but he just used his helicopters to save you from the NSA."

"I thought those were FBI agents."

"The FBI is a bit behind. Your problem is all the NSA agents."

"The NSA has agents?"

"According to Booker, the NSA has an army of assassins and spies. They don't just crunch data anymore, they use it."

"It takes a snake to know a snake," Gale sneered. "But if Booker's right about the NSA, then they are the ones who killed Rip. That means they have the Eysen now."

"Gale, I should have told you as soon as we picked you up," Larsen said sheepishly.

"What?" she asked, alarmed.

"The news report about Rip is bogus."

"What's that mean?"

"He's alive," Larsen said, grinning. "Rip is alive and free."

Her face lit with an elated smile. She laughed for a second, and then turned angry. "Are you sure?"

"Yes."

"Where is he?"

"We don't know exactly."

"Turn this thing around. Take me back to Flagstaff."

"We can't do that Gale."

"Get Booker on the phone. I want to return to Arizona. That son of a bitch knew when I called him, didn't he?"

"I don't know what he knew."

"Bull! Why are you being so loyal to Booker?"

"Booker wants the same thing I do. He's trying to protect Rip, you, and the Eysen."

"Booker doesn't give a damn about me. He's only helping Rip because he wants the Eysen."

"If that's true, why did you call him?"

"Because the Eysen is more than an eleven-million-year-old super-computer, but in order to prove that, to find its full potential, it needs to be understood."

"And you think Booker understands it?"

"Yes. I think Booker understands a lot more about all this than he's telling. But that's not why I called him. I need money and protection, lots of both, to find the answers. Booker is the only one who can provide that."

"What about Senator Monroe?"

She stared at him as if slapped. "So, he told you too?"

"It was a long time ago. I don't care."

Gale suddenly realized that Larsen still thought they might be a couple. "Larsen, look, a lot has happened since you and I last saw each other. You and I . . . how can I put this?" She looked across the small cabin table. "Do you remember that we were about to call it quits the day we found the Eysen?"

"We were?" Larsen asked, looking hurt.

"Yes. And even though we never got the chance to talk, it has to be over between us. I mean, let's please stay friends, but that's it. I'm sorry. Okay?"

Larsen stared at her a moment. "You fell for Rip, didn't you?"

"You're kidding. What is it with men? I decide not to go out to dinner and dancing with you and it's because I'm interested in someone else? Did it ever occur to you that I've been too busy running for my life and I don't *want* a boyfriend at the moment?"

"All right Gale," Larsen said, in his best calm voice. "We're friends. More than that, we've all risked everything to protect the Eysen. We have no idea where it is, or even exactly what it is, but you've spent days studying it. Why don't you tell me what you learned?"

"I can't."

"Why not?"

"Because I don't know your motives."

"You don't know . . . I *found* the damned thing. Do you realize that Gale? Rip and I looked for proof of Cosega for years, but in the end *I'm* the one who found it. Then he steals it and runs into the night. All this could have been different."

"That's my point Larsen. You still think Rip made a mistake. You think he caused all this death and mayhem when in fact, everything that has happened proves he was right."

"I'll admit that, but for someone who is as close to Senator Monroe as I understand you are, to question *my* motives is pretty incredible. Why aren't you with Rip anymore anyway? How did you get separated?"

"Ask Booker."

"I'm asking you."

"Booker told him about Monroe and me. After finding out about you and me, and then Sean's betrayal, it was all he needed to remember he didn't like me from the start."

Larsen nodded.

"I mean it. I wasn't going to talk to Booker. Sooner or later this thing will have to land, and when it does I'll call Monroe if I have to, but I'm going back to Arizona."

Harmer walked up and took the seat across the aisle from Gale. "We just got word. Rip was on a small plane that took off from an airstrip outside Flagstaff a few hours ago. An FBI agent and one of the Vatican's men were killed." She tapped a cigarette on the armrest, flipping it over and starting again, knowing she couldn't light it.

"Where'd the plane go?" Gale asked.

"We don't know yet."

"Why should I believe you?"

Harmer rolled her eyes. "Don't."

8

An FBI agent showed up at Barbeau's hotel room. He'd just watched a report on Gaines' death, and was mystified at the blatant propaganda the NSA was using, but for whose benefit?

"Special Agent Dixon Barbeau?"

"Yeah."

He identified himself as an agent for DIRT, the FBI Director's covert unit. "Would you mind coming with me, sir?"

Barbeau put on his shoes and followed the agent. The elevator was busy, so they took the stairs, three fights. As soon as they reached the parking lot, the agent handed Barbeau a phone.

"Do you want to tell me what happened?" Barbeau recognized the FBI Director's voice.

"I already reported the shooting to the Office of the Inspector General under Order 2492, and I've also advised the Civil Rights Division's Criminal Section of the incident. In light of Agent Hall's death, there should be no question that my use of lethal force to stop Leary was justified."

"Damn it, Dixon, the phone is scrambled. I don't want the damned official version. Tell me what in the name of hell possessed you to let Gaines go?"

Barbeau was surprised by the question. Although he trusted

the Director about as much as he could trust anyone involved in this case, he'd been planning to keep him in the dark about what really happened. "What do you know?"

"I know that I'm still considering getting on the red-eye and coming out there to take your badge so I can personally see the look on your face when they slap the cuffs on you for obstruction of justice, aiding and abetting a fugitive, and murder."

"Murder?"

"I've seen the film. Did you warn Leary?"

"If I'd warned Leary, Gaines would be dead. Maybe even me."

"And if you'd warned him, maybe Gaines wouldn't have gotten away. And that wouldn't have been any good, would it? What the hell were you thinking? Tell me something really good Dixon, because I've got four DIRT agents standing in the parking lot ready to take you in."

Barbeau had already spotted them. The Director actually thought he might resist. It was astonishing. But the real surprise was the film. He knew the NSA had satellites that could do that, but that meant they knew exactly where Gaines was, and they had also let him go.

"You yourself told me that if we brought Gaines in, 'the artifacts will disappear either to Rome or to the NSA. Then, Gaines would be killed in a staged suicide.' I believed you, and thought we needed more time."

"Jesus! Are *you* the Director? Why do you think *you* get to make that call? Your job was to *apprehend* the suspect. You don't get to decide what happens next. That's well above your pay grade."

"I decided I could not safely bring in the suspect. If you need to charge me, do it."

"Don't tempt me," the Director said. Neither spoke for a moment. "You should have discussed it with me."

"It wasn't premeditated. I saw Leary kill Hall and couldn't stop it, but I could save Gaines. Seeing what the Vatican was willing to do and knowing the NSA was actively blocking us, it just all suddenly came together. Hall never believed Gaines was the bad guy in this case. I guess I finally agreed with him. He essentially died to protect that damned artifact. I wasn't ready to just let it wind up in the hands of those who killed him without first knowing what it is."

"I'm sorry about Hall, he was a good man," the Director said. "But you have no idea how big a mess this has put us in. The NSA has film of the lead investigator in the case letting the suspect go. They gave it to Attorney General Dover, and he shared it with the Vatican. The President is getting pressured from three sides, and he and Dover have been all over my ass for the past two hours."

"The NSA let Gaines go."

"Hell, I know that."

"Has anyone asked *them* why?"

"No one cares what the NSA does. The Vatican figures the longer it takes for the NSA to get Gaines, the more chance they have at him too. Dover and the President are doing what the NSA wants, so if they think it's best to let him run around loose a little longer—"

"Just don't let a lowly Special Agent make a decision."

"Something like that. The thing is, Dover wants you off the case."

"He's the boss," Barbeau said. "I don't mind getting on with my life."

"He may be my boss, but he doesn't run the Bureau. He may even want the NSA to get the thing so he doesn't have to deal with the Vatican. But my guess is he'd rather get it first, so he can be in the position to demand favors from whomever he wants."

"Still, I'm in the way."

"Maybe not. You are the agent most familiar with this case. That means you have the best chance to resolve it."

"That's your call. But if I'm continuing, I'll need some answers. Like why is the NSA lying about Gaines's death?"

"Probably trying to throw off the Israelis and any other interested parties."

Barbeau was surprised to learn that more groups were coming after the Eysen. "Where is Gaines?"

"No one is saying, but we'll get an answer soon. The bigger question is where is Gale Asher?"

"I assumed the NSA had her," Barbeau said. "Any idea why she and Gaines split?"

"No. And Dover just asked me what leads we had on her, so if it's safe to assume the Vatican is still looking," the Director explained.

"What about Booker or Senator Monroe? They could be helping her disappear."

"DIRT is working both. Booker is damn near impenetrable, but we're making some progress."

"Then our best hope is to get Gale Asher before the NSA does."

9

Gale agreed to wait for Booker, mainly because she didn't have enough money to return to Flagstaff, and she believed Rip was long gone. Even if he were still there, she didn't know where to look. Any chance she had to find him depended on a man she couldn't stand and didn't trust. Booker Lipton.

They'd arrived at sunset. The private home was located high in the hills above Taos, in an exclusive area just south of town known as the Stakeout. There had been barely enough room for the large helicopter to land.

Where would Booker's set down? Gale wondered.

"That's a million dollar view," Gale said, standing on the large deck.

"Closer to four million I'd guess," Larsen said as they looked out across the Rio Grande Gorge, which split the expansive mesa so dramatically that one could almost see the cataclysmic upheaval as the earth tore apart.

"Booker has been delayed. He'll be here about six a.m. You might as well settle in for the night," Harmer said, lighting up a cigarette.

"What's more important than this?" Gale asked, annoyed.

Harmer shrugged.

Kruse stopped scanning the hills below them through his riflescope. "Listen Gale, you may not realize it, but we've gone to a lot of trouble to find you, get you, and protect you. I have no idea why Booker will be late, but I can tell you this. That was the NSA back there in Flagstaff. They had you under high-surveillance, and the FBI is even more interested in detaining you now that Rip has vanished. Both of those agencies know Booker has you. He'll be lucky to avoid arrest himself, so if it takes him a few more hours to get to this remote corner of the world you chose, then I think you should quit whining and cut him some slack."

She looked to Larsen for some support. He gave her only a slight nod, as if to say he agreed with Kruse. "Forgive me for not having confidence in you," she said, turning back to Kruse, "but you let Rip get away. You had ten days to get him and you couldn't do it."

"We got you out," Harmer said.

"Only because I called."

"Look, I'm sure you think you're smarter than the rest of us," Kruse said, "but we're not dealing with the Boy Scouts here. The NSA, the FBI, and the Vatican Secret Service are three of the most advanced agencies in intelligence and law enforcement in the world. You're damned lucky we got you. Hell, you're lucky to be *alive* right now!"

"Gale, they're right," Larsen said. "We're still in danger."

"Yeah, let's talk about danger," Kruse snapped. "The Vatican has a kill order on you. That means there are thousands of agents around the world who are searching, and will shoot to kill you on sight. The NSA hasn't arrested you because they are still hoping you'll lead them to the Eysen, and the FBI, under the Attorney General, seems to be working for the Vatican, so you can guess what will happen when they find you."

"I know my situation isn't good," Gale said. "All I'm asking for is honesty."

"I'm happy to give you honesty, honey. All those people I just told you about . . . they *are* out there. They *are* coming. And they may find us tonight."

"And until our backup arrives tomorrow," Harmer said, crushing a cigarette under her foot, "we're the only thing standing between you, and death or prison."

"I get it," Gale said, storming into the house. She found a bathroom and locked herself in it.

She wanted to cry, but couldn't. All her tears had been used up and wasted on Rip's death. Gale wasn't even positive that Booker wasn't holding her prisoner. What would happen if she demanded to be taken into town? It didn't matter, she knew there were too many people looking for her. Leaving now would be suicide.

Booker was her only hope. She came back to Taos to finish what she'd started with Rip. Understanding the Cosega Sequence was going to take more than just the Eysen. Clastier knew far more than that the Church was wrong. He'd seen an Eysen, had understood it, and she suspected it had been the source for his Divinations. Those prophecies had been too accurate.

She checked her pack. The Papers were safe. Her journal had many notes about Clastier and everything Rip had ever said. Circled in one of the margins was the thing she was counting on most – the letters to Trampas. Opening her wallet, she counted her remaining cash – eight dollars. Three credit cards would only buy her a one-way ticket to prison.

If she were going to succeed in filling in the gaps from Clastier's story, she would need more than Booker's money and protection. She might have to trust Larsen. She knew he was a good guy.

As long as Booker hadn't corrupted him.

10

Saturday July 22nd

Rip hardly remembered crawling into bed the previous night. He opened his eyes and was immediately assaulted with bright sunlight, reaching for his pack next to him. Reaching in, he found the Eysen. It was nearly noon, at least in whatever time zone he'd last adjusted his watch. He didn't even know where he was. The sun's warmth made him want to dive right into the Eysen. He could actually do it in bed if he wanted, but it would have to wait.

Rip had been through too much to be impatient. He needed to know his exact location and his best escape options, should they be necessary. He looked out of the window and saw nothing but trees and a distant ridgeline.

Slinging his pack over his shoulder, he wandered out into the rest of the single-level house. Saltillo-tiled floors led him into another bright room that was three times the size of his bedroom. Dyce and Elpate were playing poker, and the only smell stronger than marijuana was coffee. He hoped there was real food somewhere.

"Hey, man, you were tired, no?" Elpate said. "You slept like three weeks!"

"Where are we exactly?"

"Central Mexico. A little village outside San Miguel de Allende," Elpate said. He held out a joint in Rip's direction. "Want a hit?"

"Does anyone know I'm here?"

"Your dad doesn't even know," Dyce replied.

"Thanks guys," Rip said. "Food?"

Elpate pointed to the kitchen where Rip found abundant avocados, tomatoes, peppers, onions, cheese, beans, and tortillas among other fruits and vegetables. They convinced him to try a drink that was half herbal tea and half cactus and lime-juice. He loved it.

After his meal, he returned to his bedroom, which opened to a small patio. He now knew the layout of the place, a three-bedroom hacienda. He was in the guest room while Dyce was staying in the room that Elpate used as an office. Rip felt safe here. At least as safe as he'd felt since leaving the dig site.

He pulled out the Eysen and set it in the sunlight. This would be his first solo view, and the excitement of being able to study the artifact uninterrupted until sunset made him almost giddy. It was only when he thought about Gale, while the Eysen initiated the Cosega Sequence, and again his mood fell.

Preparing for a long study session, Rip powered up his laptop, made sure the wireless connection was off, and brought up the photos of the casing. They momentarily sent his mind back to Asheville. Was the house still standing? Were the casing and the original Clastier Papers still hidden in the secret room behind the shelves?

He pulled out the Odeon and studied it in the sunlight as he recalled that moment on the trail when Larsen had handed it to him. It had been the first artifact to come from the cliff before it yielded the stone globe casings that contained the precious Eysen. Ever since, he'd hardly had a chance to consider it. The Odeon seemed static and mute next to the dynamic Eysen. Still, it must be important. Surely it hadn't been inadvertently left there. No doubt remained that the Eysen, protected by the stone casings, and the Odeon, were intentionally preserved. The Eysen might appear to function like a computer, but it was first and foremost a time capsule.

During that first night, when they had run through the forest from the dig site, he'd briefly thought about the Odeon and wondered if it would light up as well, but the Eysen was too incredible, and had demanded all his attention. Now, however, it was a key piece of the puzzle.

There was an old Indian saying, *"The questions are found in the answers. And until you know what the questions are, you cannot understand the answers."* It meant different things to different people, but he'd adopted it for archaeology, meaning that in order to understand the whole site, each artifact must be studied until it surrendered not just its answers, but also the questions to ask of the next artifacts.

Turning the Odeon in his hands, the flat, nearly perfect oval shimmered in the sun. Although only about the size of a bar of soap, the pearly finish made it seem bigger. Nearly translucent, the quartz-like substance had three inlaid gold lines – almost identical to the ones on the casing. Yet its simple elegance reminded him of the Eysen.

The epiphany hit him – hard. He felt like a fool for not realizing it before.

"It must open," he whispered to himself.

As soon as Pisano, the dapper Vatican representative, learned of Leary's death and Nanski's arrest, he demanded a meeting with Attorney General Dover. A high-level Vatican official had already phoned the President, but thus far had not been able to speak with him.

"We will be lodging a formal complaint," Pisano said while trying to understand how the Attorney General could wear *that* shirt with *that* tie. He was curious as to what Dover did with his money, because it certainly wasn't spent on clothes. The man would never be President.

"I doubt that a formal complaint will be filed," Dover said. "Seeing how most of the world has no idea our Church employs gentlemen such as yourself, Joe Nanski, and the late Mark Leary, the prudent public relations move would be to let it go."

"When will Nanski be released?"

"Within the hour."

"Why is it taking so long?"

"He was arrested at the scene of a fatal shooting of a federal agent. Do you realize that Leary needlessly killed a decent man who was just doing his job?"

"I'm sorry, but he was interfering with *our* objectives. Leary is in the presence of God now, and will be judged by the only One who can make a determination of who and why someone deserves to die. Need I remind you, it is His plan?"

"I don't need a lesson in theology from you," Dover said, wanting Pisano out of his office. "My faith in God and my loyalty to His church are not in question."

Pisano found a hair on his pants. He looked around, horrified that someone might have seen it. "Do you have a cat?" he asked, disgusted, while glancing suspiciously under the desk.

"No, I don't have a cat," Dover responded, puzzled. "Now, if there is nothing else, I'm late for a meeting."

"Yes, there are two more things. We want Dixon Barbeau taken off the case and charged in the Mark Leary death."

"The decision to charge him will be made by an internal investigation. There are procedures for this and I cannot, and *will* not, interfere. Whether he will remain on the case or not is under review. I make no promises."

Pisano scowled, but decided not to argue. "And the second point is that we must be allowed to interview Gale Asher as soon as she is apprehended, which I assume is just hours away now."

"I've just spoken with the FBI Director and she is still at large. Rest assured, she is among our highest priorities. We have considerable resources throughout the government assigned to the task of finding and arresting Gale Asher."

"And we'll have an opportunity—"

"I will see to it that you get as much time as you need to question her."

"We need to be involved from the beginning. That is to say, we have to be present at the initial, and all subsequent interrogations. We are further requesting that Joe Nanski be allowed to question her, alone, as early as possible."

"I'll consider that request."

"Please do. Expect a call from Rome as soon as we get word

of her arrest." Pisano smiled. His hope was that Vatican agents would find her long before the Bureau, but he needed all possible outcomes covered. The Vatican was working diligently to find a solution to its biggest problem: Booker Lipton.

12

Barbeau had allowed the most sought after fugitive in the world to escape. It had been a spontaneous decision that he spent surprisingly little time second-guessing. In spite of his differences with Hall, he respected the dead agent so much that his theories of the bizarre case had crept into his own, and Barbeau could now no longer differentiate them.

For the moment Gaines was lost to him, but he expected to get another chance once he knew more, when it was safer. The three greatest lessons he had learned as an investigator were written on a folded slip of yellow paper in his wallet. He took it out whenever things looked bleak, and invariably he'd see something he had missed. The DIRT team was waiting in the chopper. He had to let them know where he wanted to go. As he prepared to check out of his room, Barbeau read his faded words:

1. Coincidences are suspicious; find enough of them and you'll solve any case.

2. The motive is either money, power, or passion, but it's really always money.

3. Crimes are a conspiracy; in addition to the suspect, there is usually someone else who can be used to unravel them.

All three rules applied to every investigation, and he had spent considerable time thinking about each of them over the past twelve days. But in this case, at this moment, it was rule number three that demanded his attention – Gale Asher.

He boarded the FBI chopper, recalling his landing in a similar one in the middle of the Jefferson National Forest, unaware his life was about to be forever changed. He remembered Hall's tension at having to work with him again. It was mutual, because Hall challenged him and Barbeau didn't like that. Not because he was insecure, on the contrary, he just didn't like to waste his time explaining himself to those he felt had inferior minds, like most of his coworkers.

"Take me to Taos, New Mexico," Barbeau told the pilot. As the helicopter rose into the air, Barbeau hardly noticed the view to the south of Sedona's red rocks bursting out of the surrounding ponderosa pine forests.

An agent handed him a file folder. It was a summary of everything DIRT knew about the Vatican's interest in the case, and it included every shred of information linking the churches Gaines and Asher had visited. Just as Hall had known Gaines was not the bad guy in this case, Barbeau had thought all along that one of the keys to this mess could be found in the churches of San Francisco de Asís, the Taos Pueblo, and El Santuario de Chimayó. He suspected that if Gale Asher were still in the country, she just might be in Taos, and if not, at least the answers she and Gaines had sought, and that he desperately needed, would be there.

13

Rip held the Odeon and carefully twisted. Nothing. Larsen must have inspected the artifact before Rip arrived at the dig site, but he hadn't mentioned anything. He thought back on the casings. What had made them open? The Eysen had so quickly taken all the attention that they'd never had a chance to study the mechanism, but he recalled something that was similar to magnets. There hadn't been latches, but maybe . . . as he manipulated the Odeon in the way he had done the casings, back and forth between his hands, the center band suddenly split.

"Eppur si muove," Rip whispered, quoting Galileo's purported defiant phrase, "and yet it moves," against the Church that forced him to recant his belief that the Earth moves around the sun.

The two halves of the Odeon revealed a small opening. A smooth, round, bluish-black stone, slightly smaller than a poker chip and nearly as thin, slid into his hand.

"And what secrets do you hold, little Odeon Chip?"

As Rip tested to see if it was pliable, the chip changed color at its center and left an outline of his thumbprint in yellow. The lines glowed so brightly that, as he held its edges, intense rays of light emanated. He moved the chip toward the wall and it projected a tiny image of his thumbprint. It could be made bigger when he pulled the chip back, but the room was too bright and the image faded.

Thinking it might be some kind of activator, he looked for a slot in the Eysen to slip the chip into, even though he knew the surface of the sphere was solid. When nothing else came to mind, he set the Odeon Chip down and placed the Eysen on top of it. To his surprise, the two ancient artifacts seemed to repel one another like opposing magnets. The result left the Eysen suspended nearly two inches above the chip.

"Whoa," Rip exhaled. His entire career had been devoted to studying dusty, often broken, objects from the past, but the Eysen and the Odeon Chip were interactive, futuristic-like artifacts that were beyond belief. *No wonder there are so many people after these things*, Rip thought while nervously looking out the window.

Suddenly the Eysen began to spin. Still suspended above the chip, it rotated counter clockwise, slowly at first. As its speed increased, he saw the Cosega Sequence run backwards. Circles and dashes rushed by in a flurry, then, moving like currents, swiftly streamed around the globe.

He looked under the Eysen and saw the chip was reflecting the images and Sequence symbols from the sphere above, except that his thumbprint, still glowing yellow, was unchanged. Then, out of the top of the Eysen, in the bright sunlight still flooding in his windows, a six-inch holographic figure emerged. As it spun around to face Rip, he was stunned beyond all reason. He recognized the image.

"Eleven million years old," Rip whispered while staring at the figure, an exact miniature replica of himself. Before he could react, the figure began peeling away layers of itself – skin, muscles, veins, bones, until all that remained at the core was a glowing beam. "Was it Energy? The human soul? Connection?" he queried aloud while checking again to make sure that his door was locked.

Within the Eysen the Cosega Sequence had stopped, as if waiting. Everything stayed suspended. He didn't know what to do. More out of nervousness that someone could see into the windows than wanting to block the sun, Rip pulled the curtains closed. They were stiff and dusty, appearing as if they hadn't been drawn in years. Elpate's house was secluded, and Rip couldn't see anything but wilderness, but he felt as if someone were watching. He'd had that feeling often since his teen years, when he always worried that his being a descendent of Clastier's church builders would be discovered. However, in the past twelve days, his fears had magnified, and had even been justified.

He turned back to the Eysen, expecting it might be dark. Instead, it glowed brighter than ever. The Cosega Sequence started again, the Earth spinning among swirls of circles and dashes, but this time it went farther back. The planet became a fiery mass, a ball of molten lava spinning through space, getting smaller and smaller. Thousands of meteors and comets that had pelted it flew out of the Earth. Riveted, perhaps not even breathing, he watched the Earth's formation as if he were seeing an old movie run backwards. Rip had studied geology and seen many simulations of the planet's formation, but nothing this vivid and detailed.

As the reversing continued, the core-earth shrank further and began breaking into smaller planets. Eventually, there was nothing but space, and even that moved back in time at incredible speed until there was nothing but a single light in the middle of the Eysen. The remaining beam floating above the Eysen that had been the holographic image of himself shot down into the center of the Eysen. His figure became part of the final point of light, so intense Rip could barely look directly at it.

The light radiated a halo rainbow of vivid colors and became brighter. Like looking into the sun, it hurt his eyes. At its final burst, the intensity was so piercing that it made him cry out in pain. Then, it went dark. The room seemed completely devoid of light, and for a few scary moments Rip thought he might be blind.

When he finally refocused on the Eysen, he could see that it was still faintly illuminated, or perhaps was slowly coming back from its blackness. Every time he'd looked into the Eysen it had surprised him. But the image that emerged before him now might have been the most shocking of all.

14

Gale had slept surprisingly well and was up waiting on the deck when Booker arrived just after sunrise. She had met many powerful and wealthy people during her time as a reporter for *The Wall Street Journal*. However, she was unprepared for the presence of Booker Lipton.

He strolled onto the deck in a cream-colored linen suit, tailored to perfection, with an air of absolute control, yet totally inviting at the same time. His disarming smile warned of his charm, but even that seemed to expand out of some hidden intensity that hung like an aura around the man who appeared fueled by pure mystery, both impenetrable and magnetic at once.

"Gale, please forgive me for keeping you waiting." He took her hand and stared into eyes even bluer than the photos he'd seen of her. "A great distance needed to be crossed and I've been moving every moment since we spoke in an effort to reach you as soon as possible."

She'd been planning on blasting him about not telling her that Rip was alive while she was still in Flagstaff. Instead, she thanked him for coming.

"We've much to discuss," he said, releasing her hand and walking to the railing. He took in the view as if he'd never seen it before. "There are *places*," he said after a moment, "and Taos is one of them, don't you agree?"

"Yes. It's quite special."

He nodded. "Tell me why you insisted upon returning here. Not the safest place for someone being sought by so many."

"I have unfinished business."

"Clastier?" he asked.

"I just need some cash, a scrambled satphone, and a car," she said, refusing his bait.

"Really?" He reached into his suit pocket and handed her a set of car keys. "Take mine. It's in the driveway, a phone on the front seat. And here . . ." He pulled a folded stack of bills from another pocket. "There should be four or five thousand there. Is that enough?"

She took the keys and the cash without taking her eyes off him. "And I can go?"

"Of course. I'm not holding you. I'm trying to help you."

"I don't trust you."

Booker laughed loudly. "I hadn't noticed," he said, then he continued laughing.

"Did I say something funny?" she asked, uncomfortable.

That just made him laugh even more. "I'm sorry Gale, but you say it as if it's a new idea. Nobody on the planet trusts me."

"How did the FBI find us in West Memphis?"

"They traced the rental car. But you have to realize that the average citizen has no privacy left. The government hears everything, even inside your house, offices, or hotel rooms."

"How?"

"What does every home, hotel room, and office have?" Booker asked

"I don't know," Gale said.

"The NSA uses advanced nanotechnology implanted in smoke detectors to monitor building interiors. They know everything."

"I don't think that's technically possible."

"You have no idea what's technically possible. But I can assure you, it is."

"How do you know?" Gale asked.

"I sell them the stuff. My companies manufacture the 'sensor' that goes into every detector."

"Another reason not to trust you."

Booker laughed again. "But that doesn't mean we can't be friends. You and I have common interests."

"Maybe *some* common interests, but very *different* goals."

"We both want Rip safe, the Eysen protected, and Clastier's words to survive."

"You want the Eysen for yourself," Gale said defiantly.

"Ultimately, I do want everything for myself, but not because I am selfish or greedy, as many think. It is because I trust so few people, and I trust only myself completely. No one else can handle the Eysen."

"You're an egomaniac."

"No. It only appears that way. Actually, I am anything but."

"Really? What would you do with the Eysen if you had it?"

"Tell me about the Eysen," Booker said.

"Let's just say you're going to have to earn my trust."

"You should trust me, Gale. You may not believe it, but I'm the best chance that good has in prevailing over the mess the world has become."

"It only appears that you're an egomaniac, huh?"

"The Eysen has the power to change everything. It has been prophesized by Malachy and Clastier. You have seen it, held it—"

"Are you envious?"

"The empty man who walks among the merchants, the state, and the church will be killed . . ." Booker said, quoting one of Clastier's five remaining Divinations. "I've always assumed I was the empty man," Booker said.

"So you have read the Papers?" Gale asked softly. It was impossible to hide her surprise.

He stared at her silently for a moment, concerned his admission had been too soon. Then he relaxed, excited at the opportunity to finally discuss Clastier. "Yes."

"How did you read Clastier without Rip knowing? Or did he know?"

"He didn't know. I couldn't let him find out I'd seen them. It had to be his quest or he'd be suspicious of me. He had been raised in the paranoid shadow of the descendants of the original Clastier Church builders. I needed him to trust me."

"But you never were trustworthy."

"You are wrong."

She considered him for a moment, thought about challenging him again, but instead sought more information. "Why do you think you are the empty man in the Divinations?"

"I walk among the merchants, the state, and the Church."

"But you are a merchant," she said. "It is Senator Monroe who is the empty man."

"Monroe? He is the state."

"But he's not. Monroe is a teacher."

Booker seemed surprised. He had not considered that. Ever since his first reading, he had assumed that he was the empty man. Clastier had been clear that his Divinations were never to be discussed until the prophecies had passed. Booker had adhered to the rule until now. What if it were Monroe instead of himself?

"Did you see anything in the Eysen to confirm this?"

"No."

"But I am hated. The NSA, the politicians, the Church, even in the corporate world, I have far more enemies than friends."

"Do you?" she asked sarcastically.

Booker nodded seriously. "Whereas Monroe has carefully crafted alliances and brokered favors for almost two decades. Why would someone assassinate him? Who would do it?"

"You know why."

Booker was silent. Of course he knew. "Because the dumbass wants to keep it himself."

"Yes."

"But so do I," Booker admitted.

"But you are a merchant, and therefore cannot walk among them. You walk as one of them."

Booker wasn't convinced. When does a man become what he is? How did Clastier see it? Certainly anyone would consider Monroe part of the state. Booker hadn't been born a merchant. Or, maybe he had. His father had been a salesman, his mother a broker – definitely merchants by Clastier's era's definition.

"What did Monroe's parents do for a living?" he asked.

"His mother was an elementary school teacher, his father a journalist, why?"

Booker was afraid to trust it. Monroe's parents were clearly not of the state, the church, or the merchants. Maybe the death sentence of the Divinations wasn't his. "Who would kill the Senator? The NSA loves him, the Vatican is supporting his every move, even our modern merchants, the corporations, are backing his candidacy."

"You might kill him."

Booker looked mildly offended. "Not me."

"It could be anyone. Everyone who learns of the Eysen will want it. Many would be willing to kill for it."

"But why kill Monroe?"

"He must be the one who winds up with it."

Booker nodded, but remained silent as he stared toward Taos Mountain. "Then you've got to meet with Monroe as soon as possible."

15

The FBI Director met Senator Monroe at the famous Chevy Chase Country Club, frequented by politicians and the "old guard" of Washington, D.C. It was the kind of place where the powerful, the famous, and newsmakers could blend in and not be bothered. But even there, Senator Monroe's charisma and the widely accepted presumption that he'd be the next U.S. President drew polite stares and greetings from wannabes and glad-handers. They finally broke free and took a golf cart out to the edge of the championship golf course, a section where Monroe had lost too many balls into the rough.

"Your meeting, Senator," the Director said, once he'd scanned the area for signs of life.

"You do realize that the NSA has Gaines?" Monroe asked.

The Director nodded. "I think they've thought that before. My agent calls him Houdini."

The Senator snapped and waved his finger at the Director. "Oh, yeah? Well Gaines isn't going anywhere. They're watching him too closely."

"Still, it's risky," the Director said, annoyed by the Senator's constant finger-snapping. He reminded him of a car salesman. "Why not just bring him in?"

"That's the plan. They just need him to figure out the Eysen first."

"A mistake, but fine with me. It just gives my people more time to get him. Where is he?"

The Senator's laughter was accompanied by a string of his rapidly snapping fingers. "Here's why we're here," he said, suddenly turning serious. "The Bureau is making things difficult for people it shouldn't: me, the current President, my friends at the NSA, my other friends at the Vatican. Why don't you go and find some real criminals? Leave the professor to us."

"What kind of criminals would you have me go after? Maybe the ones you just listed? I mean, Senator, if I can't arrest any of your friends or associates, the Bureau might as well just close its doors."

The Senator snapped once but didn't laugh this time. "Okay, J. Edgar, you think this is a power trip. Let me tell you what real power is and what it can do. The world is full of bad people who want to change things to something ugly. The American way is the way. Catholicism is the true religion. Do you think I chose these paths by accident? I shopped around. I'm on the right side."

"Your way or the highway?"

"I'm just trying to warn you, really just tell you: don't go the wrong way." He stepped back and looked at the Director as if trying to decide if he was worth his time. "Listen to me. Do you want to have a job in my administration?"

"In the event you survive the primaries and go on to win the general election—"

"In the event . . ." the Senator snapped in the rhythm of a rimshot. "You're good for laughs, I'll grant you that, but your naïveté scares me. The primaries are so that ordinary politicians with big egos think there is a process and believe they may have a chance at becoming president. The general election is so that the American people think they are in control and believe there is a choice."

"Maybe I'm not as cynical as you," the Director said. "Regardless, if you win, we both know you're not going to keep me."

"No, I wouldn't leave you as head of the Bureau. Clearly I'm not an idiot. But we'll find something for you in Homeland Security. Might not be able to keep your pay grade, but maybe, depending—"

"Senator, I have no interest in working in your administration, but I'll remember your generous offer."

Monroe looked off to the woods, seemingly distracted. The Director wondered if someone might be out there recording the conversation. He knew that even if the Senator weren't trying to set him up, someone in Washington was always monitoring everything.

The Senator let go of whatever had been distracting him. "Okay Director, then do this." He reached into his pocket and pulled out a few papers. "I think you'll find this interesting."

The Director took the three, stapled sheets and flipped through them. "Where did you get this?"

"There you go again, being funny."

"Impressive. And you want me to . . ."

"To do your job," Monroe said, snapping both hands and firing them at the Director like two cap guns.

"You think I can bring a case against one of the richest, most powerful men in the world based on three pages of data collected by dubious sources?"

"I don't give a damn about a case, although, now that you mention it that would be nice. What I need you to do is arrest him. I have a sneaking suspicion the judge that handles the preliminary hearing will be sympathetic when the Department of Justice demands remand with no bail."

"Seems farfetched. But I'll put some people on it. If this stuff is real, I'll arrest him. That is, if we can find him."

"Don't worry, I'll let you know exactly where you can find him. You just be sure you're ready." Monroe snapped his fingers, pointed to some greenery beneath a dogwood tree, bent down, and pulled out a golf ball. "I think this is one of mine."

"Are we done?" the Director asked.

"We're finished talking for today. But we won't be *done* until I see on cable news that you've arrested Booker Lipton at the White House."

16

Deep inside the secret NSA command center in Arizona, Jaeger was as angry as his subordinates had ever seen. On a secure call, he requested approval for the assassination of Booker Lipton. "The son-of-a-bitch went in there, snatched Gale Asher from us, and vanished her into thin air," he ranted to his superior. "AX, that army of his, has suddenly become a large presence in Mexico. It's only a matter of time until they find Gaines."

"Put more agents in San Miguel," his superior said. "Booker is powerful, but he can't match our boots on the ground down there. We can move enough DEA, CIA, DHS, NSA, and other assorted personnel into the area that we'll outnumber the locals."

"It won't be enough. He's got us beat on the tech side. He makes the damn stuff *for* us. We need to implement the plan. Booker has to be terminated or we'll lose this thing."

"Then we should bring Gaines in, now. We'll get him into one of the Virginia safe-houses, bury him so deep undercover that even I can't find him."

"Then we'll never unlock the Eysen," Jaeger said impatiently.

"I'm not convinced of that. We can put a team of experts on it—"

"We've been over this. It's not just brainpower we need. According to the Vatican intercepts, only Gaines can do it." Jaeger paused. "Are you willing to risk that?"

Silence.

"We must take Booker out, *now*," Jaeger said.

"I'll talk to the President."

After the call, Jaeger dispatched orders with the efficiency of a battle commander. Booker had to be located. He had been a priority for the past week, but now more people were assigned. "He must be hunted like the snake he is," Jaeger said. "Look in the dark places, but find him!" Jaeger was confident he'd get the approval for the kill. This was a Scorch And Burn mission, after all. More personnel were moved into San Miguel, mostly as cover. Only the most elite agents could handle this case. The rest were "window dressing."

The NSA had two weaknesses he'd discussed with superiors: the finite number of highly trained employees, and reliance on outside vendors for their technology. An unknown number of those suppliers were secretly owned or controlled by Lipton-affiliated companies. No one knew just how many, but Jaeger feared the number was a dangerously high percentage.

Another weakness, far more dangerous than the other two, might also exist. Booker Lipton could be listening to the NSA. What if he knew everything we were doing, or even some of it? Those thoughts had been stealing his sleep for several nights. Booker Lipton was too dangerous to be allowed to live.

"Do you know what Genghis Khan would do in this case?" Jaeger asked his lead operative.

"Is this a trick question?" the operative asked, used to Jaeger's military strategies.

"Genghis Khan would destroy every single company Booker owns."

"Couldn't that harm the NSA? Even the entire U.S. intelligence community could suffer at the loss of his firms, not to mention defense and the U.S. lead in technology."

"That's just it. Khan would not care, because the destruction of his enemies was the source of his power. His boldness terrified the world, and through it he was able to unify vastly different tribes."

The operative stared at his boss, unsure what was expected of him.

"I'm concerned that killing Booker Lipton may not be enough. You've read the reports. This is not some ordinary businessman. He is hated and feared, ruthless and brilliant. He seems obsessed with nothing other than obtaining power."

"And the Eysen."

"Same thing."

The operative nodded hesitantly.

"I'm afraid he has some doomsday scenario that his staff will implement in the event of his death. Something that could turn the NSA and the entire Intelligence Community inside out."

"Is that possible?"

"Anything is possible with Booker's money. I'm convinced the man wants to take over the world," Jaeger said as he started to jump rope.

The operative raised an eyebrow, wondering if his tightly wound boss might just be coming a bit unwound.

"Gale Asher is vital," Jaeger said between jumps, "to keeping this thing under control. Whatever happens with Booker, we need her. Do whatever it takes to find her. Understand?"

"Yes, sir."

"I'm still not sure her split with Gaines wasn't staged." Jaeger's breathing was more labored. "Something hasn't been right about her involvement all along. Get Senator Monroe on the phone."

17

Rip stared at the Eysen, trying to process what he had seen, unable to understand how it was possible. What was this thing really?

The knock at his bedroom door sounded like a distant cannon blast. He scrambled to get the Eysen and the Odeon back into his pack and stuffed the chip into his pocket.

"You alive in there?" Dyce asked, opening the door.

"Yeah, working."

"Huh, well, you look like you need a drink." Dyce extended a glass of something strong.

"No, thanks. I need to focus."

"Yeah. We thought you'd want to see yourself being killed on TV."

Rip followed him out to the other room.

"Here it comes," Elpate said.

Rip stared as the screen showed him running, then pulling out a gun. He flinched as he watched federal agents gun him down. The aerial footage wasn't entirely clear, but it sure looked like him. They zoomed in and out, repeated the final seconds several times, before switching to a clear image of a body covered in a sheet being loaded into an ambulance.

"Dude, are you dead?" Elpate feigned concern, looked impressed at the joint he'd been smoking, then burst out laughing.

Rip was not amused.

"Why do they want everyone to believe you're dead?" Dyce asked.

"The real question is *who* do they want to think I'm dead?" Rip went over the list in his mind. Assuming it was the NSA that had faked the story, they would be hoping to convince . . . Booker? The Vatican? The FBI? Larsen? Gale? It was the last name that worried him the most. At first he felt sad that she would think he'd been killed, and that surprised him. But a bigger concern took over.

What would she do if she thought he had died? She'd go straight to Monroe with the Clastier Papers.

Would Monroe give them to the Vatican, or the NSA? The only other copies were in the secret room at the Asheville house. Even if they had survived up until now, Gale had surely told someone about them. But he had the letters and the Eysen, and the only people in the world who knew his location were in the same room.

"We need to talk," Dyce said. "How long are you planning on staying?"

"As long as I can," Rip replied, looking toward Elpate.

"Hey, it's cool with me as long as no one comes looking for you," Elpate said.

"Who is likely going to come looking?" Dyce asked.

"You saw the news. Maybe only the people who produced that little docudrama."

"Okay. I'm gonna hang for a few days to see how things go, make sure my plane is cool. Then I'm heading back to the states," Dyce said. "Elpate, you good with Rip hiding out here for a while?"

"As long as you need, my friend," Elpate said. "Unless you

start sleeping in a coffin and stuff like that." He choked out a smoky laugh.

"Thanks," Rip said, eyeing his room. "I'm going to get back to work."

"Yeah," Dyce said. "I'll come get you if there are any new developments. I'm just glad your dad knows you're really alive."

Back in his room, although anxious to get back into the Eysen, Rip hesitated. The mention of his father made him remember that his dad hadn't met them at the airstrip because he was under surveillance. The NSA would still be watching him, and looking into all his friends. How long would it take to find the connection to Dyce, then discover Dyce was a pilot, then locate his plane?

"God damn it, will I ever be safe?" Rip said to himself as he moved the curtains to look outside. "No," he whispered, shaking his head. "Sooner or later, like Clastier, they'll find me and I'll be killed because of the Eysen." He took it out of his pack. It felt heavier, the little black ball that he searched for forever and now was trapped by.

Clastier, he suddenly recalled, may have gotten away. There was no end to his story. He'd been told of rumors, of legends, that said he escaped. Maybe Rip could too.

He dug the Odeon Chip from his pocket, placed it on the table, and set the Eysen on top of it, wondering if it would return to the stunning images he'd witnessed before the interruption. Immediately, the two artifacts pushed against each other, causing the Eysen to float and spin. Then, as before, the Cosega Sequence began. Rip watched closely, as there were often minute differences. He knew the Sequence was the key not just to understanding the Eysen, but to his very survival.

Twelve hundred miles away in a darkened room at the NSA's Phoenix, Arizona command center, Jaeger watched live video feeds of the exterior of the house in San Miguel where Rip was hiding. He could also hear every word spoken inside. He'd heard them watching the news account of his death, amused they liked his work.

"Yes, Mr. Gaines. Stay put in your safe little mountain house. No one knows you're there. Well, no one except your friends at the NSA," Jaeger said, as his colleagues smiled. "But to answer your questions, no. You will never be safe. And, yes, sooner or later, you'll be killed because of the Eysen . . . my bet is that it will be sooner."

18

Gale and Larsen set out in a small, silver SUV while Kruse and Harmer followed in a white sedan. Booker had insisted his AX agents ride with Gale, but she refused. The compromise of allowing them to follow was reached only when Booker reluctantly agreed to use his contacts to find out what happened to Grinley, Fischer, and Tuke, the three ex-cons who had helped Rip and her get to Taos. She feared they were already dead, but if there were any chance they weren't and could still be saved, they deserved Booker's assistance.

Gale wasn't sure if the AX agents were there to protect her, or to make sure she didn't take off, but in the end, their presence did comfort her. "Kruse and Harmer are okay," Larsen said. "And, more importantly, they're good at what they do."

She nodded. The car had been swept for listening devices as a precaution, but Gale wasn't worried about the NSA. They didn't even know where she was. However, she assumed Booker had the car wired and would be able to hear their conversation.

"Where to?" Larsen asked, his large hands swinging the steering wheel around the tight curves. In a few minutes they would reach the main road and have to decide whether to head

north to the town of Taos, or south toward Española and
Santa Fe.

"We're going to Chimayó," Gale said. "There's a woman I
need to speak with." How she was going to get Teresa to talk to
her was something she still hadn't worked out, but perhaps
Clastier could get her in the door.

By the time they had split up, Rip still hadn't read all of
Clastier's letters, but had already seen several mentions of notes
sent to Padre Romero, whose church was located between Taos
and Las Trampas. Rip had told her that Clastier's letters to Flora
indicated that Clastier and Romero were close. He'd speculated
that those letters to Romero might also have survived. First Gale
hoped to get copies of Teresa's, and then find the ones to
Romero.

She explained it all to Larsen as they drove. She just couldn't
think of a way to keep her plans from Booker. There wasn't time
to hide everything. If she got the letters and needed to get away
later, she'd figure that out at the time. Booker still wanted things
from her, like her meeting with Monroe, so she still had things
left with which to bargain.

"So this Teresa lady sounds a little loco," Larsen said.

"Maybe. But she sure took a liking to Rip."

"Could she have sensed that Sean wasn't trustworthy? Some
people are in tune like that."

"I thought of that. But if she were that perceptive, she
should have known that Rip was also Conway."

"Who is Conway?"

"Long story. Past-life stuff."

"Oh. That's all we need."

"What's that mean?"

"We've got some sort of an eleven-million-year-old computer,
ancient prophecies, a secret antique manuscript, a Vatican
conspiracy, and the world's most dangerous spy agency involved .
. . why not add in some New Age nonsense," Larsen said.

"Nonsense, huh?" Gale considered entering into a debate.

"You damned scientists think you know everything, but all you do is look at what's visible."

"What can I say, I like to *hold* the evidence of the past. Science prefers facts. Things that can be tested, again and again."

"The great inventor Nikola Tesla said, 'The day science begins to study non-physical phenomena, it will make more progress in one decade than in all the previous centuries of its existence.' What do you think of that?"

"I'm not sure he really said that. I looked that quote up two days ago. It's attributed to him, but I couldn't find the original citation that he actually said that."

"Why were you looking up *that* quote?" Gale asked, struck by the coincidence.

"Because Booker said it to me while trying to explain some project he's working on."

"What project?"

"It's complicated. Ask him tonight." Larsen checked his rearview mirror to be sure Kruse and Harmer were still back there. "Anyway, what if the Chimayó lady won't see you?"

"Then we're going to have to break in and rob her."

"You're not serious?"

19

Attorney General Dover kept his word to Pisano's Vatican superiors and had Nanski released from the Phoenix, Arizona detention center.

Pisano ordered Nanski to immediately join the search for Gaines along with countless other Vatican agents in Mexico. Nanski refused. "Even if we can locate him, the NSA is going to be there first. Our best hope is to find Gale Asher and pursue the Clastier angle."

"I fail to see your logic," Pisano said, clicking his gold pinkie ring against the phone to punctuate his point.

"I'm not surprised. But regardless of your ignorance, I'm going to Taos."

"I'm in charge of this operation Nanski. Do as I say, or you'll be looking for another job."

Without responding, Nanski hung up and called the cardinal in Rome.

"It grows darker," the cardinal said in Italian as he answered, referencing the *Ater Dies* or "black day" when the Church would end.

"Yes, tomorrow could be *Ater Dies*," Nanski responded. "I am comforted only by the proverb, 'It is darkest before the dawn.' But I confess I am filled with fear that the sun will not rise."

"The treasure is decided."

The cardinal's words made Nanski gasp. He knew "the treasure is decided" was reference to a term used within the Church several times during the past two thousand years. It meant that the Vatican's most valuable assets and documents had been decided, and were prepared to move, perhaps already secretly being taken out of Vatican vaults and hidden elsewhere in the world.

The cardinal made arrangements to wire funds to Nanski so that he could fly to Taos, rent a car, and pursue the last fading chances to save the Church. The cardinal also told Nanski more about the *Ater Dies*, the prophesized artifact Gaines and many others called the Eysen. The revelations were shocking enough to momentarily shake the faith of a man willing to do anything for his church, its Pope, and the almighty God they worshipped.

Nanski drove in silence, in some ways glad that Leary was gone. He expected his former partner's long declared plan of raising so much hell in heaven that some newcomers would be confused had not panned out. And he had little hope that Leary could be any more helpful than he was on the earthly plane.

He tried to make sense of what the cardinal had told him.

The Eysen would power on for anyone, and even reveal considerable data. However, there were certain people – like Gaines and Clastier – who could make the black sphere do far more amazing things and discover much more. It was unclear why, but they knew this with certainty because they had two others. Nanski kept repeating the cardinal's words, trying to make himself believe them.

"Gaines has found the third Ater Dies. We have the other two. If the third is lost, so are we."

He'd only briefly explained that the first had come from somewhere in Europe, centuries before Clastier obtained the second. How could even one exist? But *three*? Why were they made? How were they constructed? Was their only purpose to destroy the Church? Nanski knew, better than most, that the Vatican was built on secrets and control as much as it was on faith and tradition, but this distorted everything.

Only when he couldn't see the road ahead clearly did he realize tears had formed in his eyes. Nanski pulled onto the shoulder and wept.

Why would God allow this? Was it a test of his faith, the world's faith? Could the Catholic Church be wrong? Wrong about . . . the origin of man? God? Everything?

Nanski cried softly, lost in a sea of doubts, a "dark night" in the middle of the day.

The few within the Vatican who had been allowed to examine the two *Ater Dies* had not been able to get very far beyond what they called the "opening routine". Still, there had been enough sporadic images over the decades that several volumes of research had been written. The information gleaned had terrified them. Although the Vatican had no idea they were anywhere close to eleven million years old, they were shocked at the technology they believed to date back a millennium.

Each Pope had been given the news on their nineteenth day in office. The ceremony was known as *Mala verba XIX,* meaning "Evil Words 19." Prior to the nineteenth day, it was thought that a new Pope would be unable to handle such horrific news. It also demonstrated that a Pope was not an absolute supreme ruler of the Church. There were others who held areas of power, kept secrets, made decisions, needed to be answered to, and it had almost always been that way. The last time a Pope cleaned house at the Vatican, kings and queens still ruled the world.

The vast, blue New Mexico sky made heaven seem far away. There was not even a breeze on the unusually still summer day to comfort him, to make Nanski feel connected and less alone. Like the calm before the storm, there was an eerie quiet in the air.

The *Ater Dies* volumes, in which each incident or image

depicted by one of the dark spheres had carefully been recorded by Vatican scholars, contained conclusions that the *Ater Dies* were inspired by divine guidance. How could something so powerful and advanced be created by man? However, the notes also concluded that the engineers who actually crafted and constructed the *Ater Dies* spheres must have made mistakes, or worse, been influenced by evil.

Nanski wiped his eyes, kissed his Saint Christopher medal, and drove back onto the highway, continuing toward Taos. How could these things be eleven million years old? The possibility that his life had been spent on the wrong path gnawed at him, testing his faith. Mile after mile, he wrestled with himself. How had these "machines" worked all these years, and why did Gaines choose the name "Eysen," the ancient word meaning to hold all the stars in your hands? He could not have known that Clastier, who had written three letters to the Pope, described the *Ater Dies* in his final one, saying, "*It is like holding the universe in your hands.*"

It was those words that caused the Pope to issue the secret decree to erase every trace of Clastier's existence.

20

Rip was disappointed that the Eysen did not return to the incredible images he'd watched before Dyce had interrupted him with the news account of his death. Instead, it showed what appeared to be an eighteenth or nineteenth century buffalo hunt by Plains Indians. The quality of the feed was superior to any high definition, the colors incredibly vivid, and, as the warriors rode, he could almost taste the dust. *How had it been filmed?* he wondered again.

Rip stopped watching in order to make notes about the earlier scenes – the most incredible he'd witnessed. He knew it was possible that the remarkable footage might never repeat, and he didn't want to lose what he'd seen.

In his writings he'd taken to referring to the people who built the Eysen as "Cosegans." Until they showed him their real name, he thought it appropriate, and thought it better than his second choice of the "Eysenites".

He typed on his laptop, *It appears the Cosegans destroyed their civilization (or it was destroyed by some outside force?) eleven million years ago. Yet the Eysen they created has shown the ability to project images from as recently as the present day. Even now I am watching events that took place in the relative recent past – a buffalo hunt of*

American Indians circa 1800. Examples have previously been noted of Sean Stadler's birth, Gale Asher's, and my own lives depicted at various points, as well as Clastier's. The most incredible had been the live feeds of Gale, Sean, and myself at Canyon de Chelly.

He paused to watch the Eysen switch from the hunt, to a battle between U.S. Cavalry and the same Indians. It was a typical slaughter as the army of the then-young nation pushed its way onto the lands that the indigenous people had called home for millennia. He couldn't stand to watch it and resumed his typing.

Today, I witnessed something beyond all previous viewings . . . He went on to describe the reverse Sequence ending in that intense light, the radiated rainbow of colors and how then everything faded, . . . *until images emerged that could only be described as a city of the future, and not just to the Cosegans, but a future far beyond our present state. Many buildings were round, super-circular skyscrapers with holes in their centers like giant doughnuts. Some appeared as figure eights, other structures like stacked coins hovering above, but not contacting the ground. There were geodesic domes and spheres, and in the air were all manner of flying machines, some blimp-like but moving with speeds that rivaled any modern jet. A few moved more slowly, and others went straight up into the heavens. I almost expected one to break through the top of the Eysen and out into my world.*

Rip read over what he'd written, frustrated by his inability to capture what he was seeing. He decided to ask Dyce and Elpate if they had a digital camera he could use to film the Eysen, or maybe they could purchase one for him. He still had plenty of cash remaining from the stash Grinley had given him.

As the massacre inside the Eysen continued, Rip tried to fathom how it could possibly show such details of the planet across millions of years. As hard as it was to understand how it could show things from millions of years in the past, it was impossible to grasp how it showed things after the Cosegans' existence, including the future beyond now. It was too extraordinary to comprehend.

It had to be documented. He should have done it before. Rip put the Eysen away and went out to ask if they had a video camera, but neither Dyce nor Elpate had one. Elpate promised he would run into town in the morning and get one. After Rip made his case, with a certain amount of pleading and his offer of an extra hundred dollars, Elpate agreed to leave sooner.

"I'm a good natured old man, happy to help you, my friend. You insult me by offering me cash like that." He smiled. "Make it two hundred American and I'll leave right now."

21

Kruse and Harmer pulled in behind Gale and Larsen in front of Teresa's house. Because it was a summer Saturday, the quiet street in Chimayó was a bit busier than usual. Larsen went back to speak to the AX agents. Gale had insisted she do this alone, mostly because Teresa didn't like crowds and a giant man like Larsen might scare her even more than seeing Gale return.

Harmer stood next to the car and lit up a smoke, giving Kruse a brief respite from the slow second-hand death she'd been inflicting on him for the last week. Larsen explained what Gale was doing, and informed them that if the old lady didn't let her inside, the three of them might be called upon to make her comply.

"Booker told us to do whatever Gale needs done. That's a blanket order, so we'll do what needs doing," Harmer said in a cloudy exhale.

"Fine. You and Larsen can handle this one," Kruse said. "I'm not a fan of beating up old ladies."

"Excuse me," Larsen said. "I don't work for Booker."

Harmer laughed. "Everyone works for Booker."

Gale knocked on the door and caught Teresa peeking out the drapes of a front window.

No answer.

She knocked again. "Please, Teresa, I have to talk to you. I need your help."

Nothing.

"Rip told me to come back here."

Nothing.

"It's about Clastier."

The door opened a few inches, a chain lock still latched.

"Could I please come in?"

"Who are those thugs on the street?"

"They are protecting me from the people after Rip and me. Look." Gale pulled out the Clastier Papers, and began reading:

"We often wonder of the true value of Life. We search for endless years as others have searched for endless ages. I am a common man. I am not trying to teach you anything, for everything written here or anywhere else is already part of you."

"You know Clastier?" Teresa asked tearfully.

"Yes."

Teresa closed the door, undid the chain, and opened it again. "There is trouble around Clastier. It was quiet for so long, but now it is worse than ever."

"I know," Gale said as Teresa triple-locked her door.

In the living room, furnished in a colonial style rather than the expected southwest motif, Gale noticed that Teresa seemed a bit disheveled and frail. "I saw on the television that Mr. Ripley was shot dead. It was those same men that came to see me who did it."

"It's not true. Rip escaped."

She frowned at Gale. "How can that be? I saw it on television."

"They made it up. It's a hoax."

Teresa seemed confused.

"He got out of the country, and he still has the copies of

Clastier's letters that you gave him," Gale said. "I need to read the originals."

"No. There's too much trouble now," she said, pulling a shawl around her neck even though the house was quite warm. "Mean men came here to scare me."

"I'm sorry. But Clastier needs us to be strong. Can I see the letters? You can look at his Papers while I read them."

"They said the Papers had been burned or lost long ago."

"See," Gale said, "they lie. The authorities don't always tell the truth."

Teresa nodded. She took the Papers from Gale. "They're not in his handwriting."

"No, the originals, in Spanish, are hidden back east. These are the English translations done many years back. But read them. You'll recognize him on those pages."

Teresa nodded and read quietly for several minutes. Tears came again. "It's him. These really are the lost Clastier Papers."

"Yes," Gale said. "Could I please see the letters?"

Teresa stood reluctantly and left the room, still clutching the Papers. Soon she returned with the letters. Once Gale found the first reference to Clastier's Eysen, she stopped reading and begged Teresa to let her keep the letters. Even though Rip had told Gale about the other Eysen, seeing it in Clastier's own words left her breathless. *A black sphere cradled within stone bowls found at Chimayó has made more of an impact on me than anything produced by the Church. Yes, it rivals even the creations of God in its wonder and grants more into the ways of its secrets . . .*

Gale spent the next thirty minutes working out a deal with Teresa. Gale would stay with her while Larsen and Kruse went to Española to copy the Clastier's letters and the Papers. Harmer would keep watch outside in case trouble came.

It was a good plan, but still Gale worried. She knew that the original Papers that had been left in Asheville were probably gone, which meant the ones she had were all that remained. Same with the letters. If Rip were captured, then only Teresa's originals would exist. Now she was essentially handing them to Booker.

She looked Larsen in the eye. "Don't let me down. These are second only to the Eysen in importance. Guard them with your life."

"Are they worth my life?" he asked.

Gale stared at him wordlessly.

"Okay," he said, nodding slowly. "Don't worry. I'll bring them back."

"I don't like smoke this close to my house," Teresa scolded Harmer. "Get back into the street with your filthy habit."

Harmer smiled at Gale. "I guess asking for a beer is out of the question."

"Git!" Teresa spat, missing the humor.

Harmer barely avoided trampling Teresa's flowers.

"She's a rude block of wood," Teresa said to Gale as they went back inside. "And a homely gal too."

Teresa made tea while they talked about Clastier, and soon Teresa revealed one last treasure that rivaled even the letters.

22

Barbeau sat in a small room, located on the grounds of the San Francisco de Asís Mission Church, just south of the town of Taos, staring at "the Shadow of the Cross," a life-sized painting of Christ done in 1896 by Henri Ault. The lights had just been turned out, yet a glowing silhouette of Jesus emerged from the darkness, his robes billowing in an invisible breeze, an aura of moonlight surrounding the moving figure as a cross and fishing boat, which had not been there before, appeared.

He'd read a brochure about the famous painting. The glowing was a mystery. Scientists who had studied the work in detail were unable to explain the phenomena. The Catholic Church did not call it a miracle, saying only that, "it is not perfectly understood." Barbeau was mildly impressed. Others in the room cried. One woman fell to her knees. And in spite of the Church's official position, several whispered, "It's a miracle."

After reading what DIRT, the FBI Director's covert unit, had come up with on the Eysen, Barbeau was ready to believe anything. The Vatican might actually be preparing for the end of the world and, oddly, Barbeau would be spending the day wandering through some of the Southwest's most celebrated Catholic churches. Ironic, he thought, moving to get a better look at the painting. Already he'd studied the altar screens in the church and spoken to anyone who might know – or even guess – why Gaines would risk so much to come there. Nothing.

Taos Pueblo did not hold good memories. They'd been so close to capturing Gaines there. Barbeau received permission to wander around the ruined San Geronimo Church. Again, he could not find anything that even connected the two places other than the Roman Catholic faith. The tour guide who had shown Gaines and Asher around had agreed to see him.

"I'm sorry to hear about Agent Hall's death," she said.

"Thank you," Barbeau said.

"And Professor Gaines is dead also. Doesn't that mean the case is closed?"

"I wish that were so," Barbeau said, sounding a little too desperate and not correcting her about Gaines. "But Gale Asher is still at large and there are many unanswered questions. Perhaps you can help. I need to know why they came here. What were they looking for?"

"I don't know. The incident with my grandfather was the only thing unusual about their visit."

"And that was certainly very unusual," Barbeau said. "What do you think that was all about?"

"My grandfather told me later that he believed Professor Gaines was the reincarnation of a man named Conway, who had ultimately been the one responsible for destroying the old church and killing all those innocent people."

"Why?" Barbeau asked, ignoring the ludicrous notion of reincarnation.

"Conway believed those in the Church were supporters of a man he was pursuing. In fact, Conway blamed the entire revolt on that man, and thought he could be hiding at the Pueblo."

"Who was the man?"

"His name was Clastier."

After getting her to spell it and then writing the name down, Barbeau asked what else she could tell him about Clastier.

"I only know the name. Before yesterday, I'd never even heard it."

Barbeau relayed the name to DIRT to research, and then tried to get the historian who had helped Gaines to talk to him on the phone during the drive to Chimayó. The historian despised Barbeau, and suggested he get a subpoena. The call was on speaker, and the agent driving the car couldn't help but chuckle. He didn't like Barbeau much either.

Not far away, also in Taos, Booker received word that the NSA had approved Jaeger's assassination request. The U.S. government had sanctioned the murder of one of its own citizens.

"This is a rather inconvenient time," Booker said to his security chief upon hearing the news.

"A three-person hit team has been mobilized," the chief said.

"Just three?" Booker asked, amused. "Where are they heading?"

"D.C., New York, and Mexico City," the chief said. "What should we do?"

"Keep tabs on them. If they get near a location I've been to in the previous twelve hours . . . kill them."

"Affirmative."

A second call came through. Booker took it and learned there was another problem. He turned to his assistant and said, "There's been a sealed warrant issued for my arrest, and the FBI means to execute. You would think the NSA and the FBI would get together on these things."

"It gets better," the assistant said, looking up from her iPad. "The President has requested your attendance at another summit on the Eysen at the White House."

Booker laughed. "Do you think they plan on arresting me or killing me there?"

"You may not be worried, but either way it's a complication we don't need."

"Damn right it is. A nasty group of complications . . . what a mess." Booker paced the room. "My bet is that Monroe is behind the arrest warrant. It would conveniently embarrass the Vice President, Monroe's opponent in the general election."

"Why bother? It's already been decided that the Senator is the next president."

"True, but Monroe would like it to be a huge victory. Or," Booker said, stopping, "Monroe might really be worried . . . not about losing the election, but about losing the Eysen." He smiled. "Tell them I'll attend the summit."

23

Elpate's return with the new digital camera could not have happened at a better time. Rip sat in his darkened bedroom watching the Eysen. It seemed to remain permanently charged now, something he attributed to the Odeon Chip, but that was only speculation.

The camera was actually a compact still camera, but it was equipped with a nice HD video feature. Elpate had been smart enough to pick up a small tripod as well and, at Rip's request, he'd gotten a stack of high capacity memory cards.

Rip had already filmed the entire opening of the Cosega Sequence. He didn't think it was the complete Sequence, which he now considered to be the Earth's rotation in the solar system, tectonic plates shifting, and endless views of wilderness along with overlaying series of circles and dashes and the complex patterns they made.

The next views presented by the Eysen were beyond belief. Rip watched what appeared to be actual visual accounts of the events described in Clastier's Divinations. He checked three times to see that the recording light was on, and then concentrated on the incredible scenes.

First a video filmed from a camera that could only have been on the seatback between President John F. Kennedy and the First Lady as they rode in the Dallas motorcade. The shots clearly came in from two angles as the graphically gruesome events were shown. Rip wondered again how it could be. Was it some sort of reenactment? How had this gotten into an eleven-million-year-old object?

The images switched again and he was on the moon, watching the first Lunar Module set down. It was filmed from the moon, before the astronauts arrived. New angles of Neil Armstrong and Buzz Aldrin walking on the surface of the moon, amazingly in the same shot, in vivid color. Who was filming them?

"Impossible," Rip said, but it kept going.

Soon he was witnessing massacres that took place a thousand years earlier during the Crusades. Next it was World War II, filmed inside a gas chamber at Auschwitz. These weren't grainy black and white newsreel footage. It was as clear as if it were happening in front of him, as if he were there.

He tried to recall all of the Clastier Divinations as the Eysen took him on a tour of world history from never-before-seen angles, providing new details and confirming historical theories. The atomic bomb destroying Hiroshima, viewed from the ground, showed horrific shots as the explosions occurred that no camera could have survived.

How did they do it?

Moving pictures in color from centuries of wars across the globe bled into one another. Da Vinci painting the Mona Lisa, Shakespeare writing, the Great Wall of China being constructed, slave ships being loaded in Africa, the images kept coming. Rip watched, fascinated, as battles from the American Civil War played out, and then Lincoln getting shot, after his assassin was purposefully let into Ford's Theatre. It expanded faster and faster until it raced as a collage of humanity's history.

When the action finally slowed to a stop, Rip was shocked to see that five hours had gone by. He'd not had food or water, hadn't eaten or drunk since the Eysen had started, but he was grateful to have been able to record it all. The camera still had about half the space left on a 128GB card.

Obviously this was how Clastier had been able to make his predications about the future. He wondered if Nostradamus, Saint Malachy, and other ancient prophets had used Eysens to peer into the future. The way they all wrote in a vague, sometimes riddle-like manner might have been because the visions were so out of context with their own times that they would have been unable to understand what they were seeing.

Rip carefully put everything away, then ventured out to the kitchen in search of a meal. Dyce and Elpate were crashed in front of the TV, a rerun of some old sitcom. Rip heated up some rice and beans, cut up some tomato, onion, and avocado, and grabbed a cold beer.

Today had been a good day, the first since he'd found the Eysen. Although no closer to decoding the Cosega Sequence, he now had the time and the tools to do it right.

Then he thought about the five remaining prophecies contained in Clastier's Divinations and shuddered.

24

Barbeau arrived in Chimayó less than ten minutes after Gale, Larsen, and their AX escorts had left. He tried unsuccessfully to get Teresa to open the door, lacking a warrant or the energy to get into another food-fight with the old lady. He headed over to the church.

He left his driver in the car while he sat in the sanctuary for more than twenty minutes. Barbeau hoped something of the church would give itself to him, not as a sign or anything silly like that. He wasn't Agent Hall. Barbeau believed in "good old-fashioned detective work." There was a good reason why Gaines had risked being captured, risked even his life, to come to all these dusty old churches in the middle of nowhere.

Maybe if he sat there long enough he would figure it out, connect the missing pieces. Chasing Gaines had distracted him from understanding the reason that he was chasing him. Hall had been right about one thing: renowned archaeologist Ripley Gaines had not taken the Eysen and other artifacts for money. Gaines knew he had something that the great powers in the world all wanted. And he believed, rightfully so Barbeau thought, that those powers would misuse whatever secrets the artifacts held.

But, why the churches? Were the artifacts religious? Was that why the Vatican had so much interest? He tracked the case over in his mind. Should he have let Gaines go? Could the Director and DIRT have protected Gaines? Would he ever get the chance to catch him again?

Barbeau felt another headache coming on, the kind that painkillers couldn't stop, but alcohol could. The problem was that "cure" only lasted a short time, and brought greater problems and lots more pain. Still, he wondered how far it was to the nearest liquor store. He recalled a neon sign in Española, "Saints and Sinners Package Liquors," an appropriate name for this case, he thought, and most assuredly they would have his brand.

He did what he always did when the lure of intoxication pulled him away from where he was supposed to be. A photo of his daughter on his phone softened him. It hadn't been just the endless rigors of the job that cost him seeing her grow up, it had been something far sneakier, damn it. She had a child of her own now. A grandson he'd never met, not even a photo.

He wandered into the room with all the crutches. There were dozens of them, wood, aluminum, hand-made, even canes, hung not abandoned and forgotten, but as a reminder. Littered among them were crosses, beads, and pictures of saints and Jesus. It was almost a tacky display, yet somehow that made it appear more authentic. What stories did this old building hold? What secrets did it hide? Gaines had come here even though the FBI and Vatican agents were minutes behind him. Why? Barbeau was driving himself insane with it. He'd let the suspect go because he had to know. What has made one of the richest men in the world, the most dominant religion, and the top spy agency of the world's lone super power, all so desperate they are killing anyone in their way?

"The NSA is so worried, they aren't even willing to bring Gaines in yet," he said to himself as he ventured back into the chapel.

His phone rang to the disapproving stares from an elderly

couple sitting in the pews. Barbeau looked at the number and quietly left the chapel.

"Clastier was a nineteenth century Catholic priest who was defrocked, excommunicated, disavowed, and actually expunged by the Vatican," the familiar voice of a DIRT agent began briefing him.

"Apparently they didn't like him much."

"No," the agent said. "There is almost nothing known. Everything we have is from intercepts. During his life, prior to disappearing in the mid-1800s, he preached at five different churches in northern New Mexico."

"Which ones?" Barbeau asked looking back at the small adobe church.

"El Santuario de Chimayó, San Francisco de Asís Mission, San Geronimo at Taos Pueblo, San José de Gracia Church, and an unknown church which was destroyed but may have been located in or near San Cristobal, New Mexico."

"Where is the San José church?" Barbeau asked about the only one still standing that he had not visited.

"Las Trampas, New Mexico."

Barbeau tapped the name into his phone and discovered the church was less than a twenty-five minute drive from his current location. While still on the phone with the DIRT agent, he told his driver where to go.

His driver looked it up. "It's kind of on the way back to Taos. We can take Highway 76, then after Las Trampas we can pick up 518 back to Taos."

Barbeau nodded, at the same time listening to the agent's voice in his ear tell him about the arrest warrant issued for Booker.

"Damn, someone sure is scared," Barbeau said. "Why did the Director do *that*?"

"Monroe brought him overwhelming evidence. The Vatican had collected enough stuff on Booker that, if we can find him, we might actually be able to convict him."

It was then that Barbeau realized that if he had taken Gaines into custody and they had tried to hide him, the NSA or the Vatican would have not only killed Gaines, but they would have silenced Barbeau as well, by whatever means necessary.

"Something else too. You remember Nanski, the Vatican's lead agent on this?"

"Yeah."

"He's in Taos."

25

Gale could not believe she was holding a second Odeon. Teresa had kept it hidden since her mother had given it to her decades earlier. Her mother had received it from her mother, who was Clastier's love, Flora. Teresa told Gale that it had been found with Clastier's "black sphere," now called an Eysen.

Larsen nearly swerved off the road when Gale showed the second Odeon to him as they wound along highway 76 to Las Trampas. "How can there be *two?*"

"There are also two Eysens," Gale said flatly.

"Should I pull over?" Larsen replied, shocked.

"No. We don't have time. I want to talk to the priest at San José de Gracia Church in Las Trampas and get back to Taos before Booker leaves."

"Booker won't leave without talking to you," Larsen said.

"Why?"

"Because nothing matters to him more in the world than the Eysen," Larsen explained. "Does he know there is more than one?"

"I don't know what he knows. But the second one was probably destroyed a hundred and fifty years ago by the Vatican."

"What are they afraid of?"

"The truth," Gale said. "As Rip says, 'People are only afraid of two things: the truth, and the unknown.' The Eysen is both."

Larsen smiled. "Yeah, I've heard him say that two or three . . . hundred times. I can't believe there is another Eysen," he said looking over at the Odeon. "That's just like the one we found in Virginia. I wonder what it does?"

"What do you mean?"

"Look what the Eysen does. We never had time to see if the Odeon does anything."

"It's in the sun right now, and nothing is happening," she said, holding it up to the windshield. "The Eysen is like a computer. . . maybe this is like a cell phone."

"Actually, it looks a little like the casing."

Gale raised an eyebrow. "You don't think?" She twisted and pulled on the two sides. Nothing happened.

"Rip was just gently moving the casing back and forth in his hands when it came open."

She tried. Three seconds later, it opened. "Oh my God!"

Larsen checked the mirror for AX. Kruse and Harmer were staying close.

"It's a chip," Gale said, holding it up to the light. The Odeon Chip did nothing. "That's disappointing." She stuffed the Chip into her pocket, closed the Odeon, put it back into her pack, then pulled out the copies of Clastier's letters.

"You're going to read now?" Larsen asked. "That's all the time you're giving that little chip? You're not much of an archaeologist."

"That's right. I'm a reporter. The Chip is a mystery I can't deal with right now. I need to know as much as I can about Clastier and Padre Romeo before we get to his church."

"He's not going to be there you know?"

"Who?"

"Padre Romero."

"My God, you sound just like Rip. I know that. But someone will be, and they may know something."

They rode in silence the rest of the way while Gale read the letters. Kruse and Harmer continued to follow closely behind.

San José de Gracia at Las Trampas, completed in 1760, was the oldest church affiliated with Clastier. "These old churches are all so beautiful," Gale said as they got out of the SUV. Kruse stayed in the car, but Harmer got out to smoke.

"Another striking adobe structure."

"The parishioners have restored and maintained it so that it looks much the same as when Clastier was here." She hurried to the door, as it was getting late. "Locked."

"Tomorrow is Sunday. We can come back then. The place will be packed," Larsen said.

"We're not tourists on vacation. I don't know if there'll even *be* a tomorrow."

Although Larsen thought the statement overly dramatic, he couldn't disagree.

A slim man in gold frame glasses, wearing an old white tee shirt, faded jeans, and a small tool belt, came around the side of the building. "Can I help you folks?" He set down several tubes of conduit and stood holding a roll of Romex wiring.

"Do you know when someone will be here?" Gale asked, smiling at the man she guessed to be in his late forties.

"Someone?"

"I was hoping to speak with someone about the church's history."

"Completed in 1760. The dozen or so families who lived in Los Trampas at that time had donated one-sixth of their paltry earnings from selling crops until they could buy enough supplies. They did all the work themselves . . . and it's still here after more than two hundred and fifty years!" He grinned. Gale couldn't tell if he was impressed with his knowledge, or the work of the original families.

"Thank you. But I meant the history of the priests who served here."

"Oh," the man said. "That's a whole different conversation."

"Do you know where I can find the priest?"

The man switched the roll of Romex to his left hand and extended his right. "I'm Father Józef Augustyniak Kowalkowski."

Gale look confused as she shook his hand.

He smiled. "Everyone just calls me Father Jak."

"I'm sorry, I thought you were an electrician," Gale said while Larsen introduced himself.

"I am today. I'm also a groundskeeper, plasterer, painter, small animal vet, and airplane mechanic."

"Wow," Gale said. "A real renaissance man."

"Well, I made up the part about being an airplane mechanic." He laughed. "Anyhow, what did you want to know about my predecessors?"

"Have you ever heard of Padre Romero, he would have been here—"

"1818 to 1851," Father Jak finished. "Yes, he was one of our longest serving priests. A great man. Why your interest?"

Gale looked at Larsen and then down to the car where Harmer was on her second cigarette. Returning her gaze to the friendly priest, she asked the dangerous question as calmly as she could since time was short.

"Have you ever heard of a man named Clastier?"

Father Jak's face registered surprise. He stared at Gale, speechless for a moment, and then handed the Romex to Larsen in order to free his hands. After digging a ring of keys from his pocket and looking over his shoulder, he simply said, "We better go inside."

26

Nanski was not shocked to see Gale Asher enter the church with the priest. Nor were the goons parked by the road entirely unexpected. He assumed they belonged to Booker. The surprise was that Larsen Fretwell was alive. How had that information not filtered back to him? The FBI, and therefore Attorney General Dover, must have known. Why keep that a secret?

It didn't matter now. Nanski had been granted a gift from God. He would not miss this opportunity.

Being outnumbered was a minor problem. If only Leary were there. But this was clearly divine intervention, and his faith was renewed. Over the last two centuries, a haphazard collection of houses, sheds, and barns had grown up around the church building. He'd been waiting in a nearby vacant barn for a couple of hours, not sure if anyone would show. He could see the car where Kruse and Harmer waited. They did not appear to be expecting trouble. Nightfall was approaching, and although that would be a better time to make his move, he couldn't risk their leaving.

He'd watched Father Jak, working on an electrical box, for more than an hour. Several times the priest had gone in and out of the back door. It wasn't locked. Getting to the old church without being seen would be a little tricky, but doable.

Nanski checked his Ruger Mark III semi-automatic pistol and shoved an extra ten-round magazine into his back pocket. His plan was to shoot Asher, Fretwell, and the priest if necessary, then wait for Booker's crew to blitz. He'd kill them too.

Gale, Larsen, and Father Jak stood inside the nave of the Church, smaller than it appeared from the outside. Only the white plastered walls and high ceiling, supported by vigas, helped expand the space. "Do you understand that the man you are speaking of never lived?" Father Jak asked.

"I didn't think priests were allowed to lie?"

He smiled and nodded. "It is true, but also a lie."

"But you know of him?"

"Yes."

"Can you tell me about him?"

"No."

"Why not?" she asked, already knowing the answer.

"It is not my story to tell."

Gale let out an exasperated sigh and walked toward the altar. The religious images everywhere seemed entirely hypocritical to her now.

Larsen told Father Jak that he was an archaeologist and Gale was a writer for National Geographic. The priest did not seem interested. He had been preoccupied ever since Gale first said Clastier's name, as if it were a secret known only to him and no one had ever said it before.

"We need your help," Gale said.

"I am at your service," the priest replied with a smile.

"Then please, tell us about Clastier," she pressed, recalling the same silly game with the historian at the San Francisco de Asís Church. "You know something that can help us and you say you will not."

His expression turned serious, and he did not speak for a full minute while he stared at the ceiling.

"How is it that you knew to come here?" he finally asked.

"Clastier knew Padre—"

"Please," Father Jak interrupted. "Consider your answer carefully. How is it you *knew* to come here?" he repeated.

Gale looked at Larson, who shrugged his shoulders. He was lost in this game of religious charades. Her answer was the same. She knew Clastier and Padre Romero were friends. She was about to say that, when she suddenly thought of how she knew that – from Teresa and Flora's letters.

"Flora sent me," she said, looking the priest in the eyes.

He breathed in deeply, nodding. The slightest smile appeared. "Please, come this way."

Nanski, waiting as long as he dared, finally began to inch his way toward the back door. In a frighteningly bit of bad timing, his phone vibrated. He crouched behind shrubbery and checked the number. Pisano again. It wasn't the first call since Nanski had hung up on him. Pisano, furious that Nanski hadn't gone to Mexico as ordered, had phoned repeatedly. As with the others, he ignored the call.

Now, past the area where Booker's people might have been able to see him, Nanski slipped into the shadows behind the church with his gun ready. His phone buzzed again. Glancing at it, he saw this time Pisano was texting. "FBI in Taos. Barbeau went to Pueblo, San Francisco de Asís, and Chimayó."

Barbeau at Chimayó could be a big problem, Nanski thought. *It's only about half an hour from here, and if Asher figured out the connection to Las Trampas, maybe Barbeau could too.*

Nanski could see the highway easily, but if Barbeau came in from Chimayó he'd be coming from the other direction. He didn't want to kill a federal agent, but he would if need be. Never once did it occur to Nanski that *he* might be killed, not because he felt invincible, but rather because he believed that God's Will would be done.

27

Exhausted, Rip readied himself for sleep. A second night in the same bed seemed an outrageous luxury. As he lay in the dark under a single sheet his thoughts were crowded. What was happening in the states? What had Booker done when Rip hadn't shown up? Where was Gale? Did Barbeau regret letting him go? Were they still watching his father?

After thirty minutes of chasing problems through his head, he got up and pulled out the Eysen.

It was a marvel to see the Eysen, set on the Odeon Chip, as it came to life and lit the room. That it worked at night was still new to him. This time he just watched the Cosega Sequence without trying to record or remember any details. Among all the zeros and dashes flowing around the evolving Earth, he detected a pulse he'd never before noticed. Its hypnotic rhythm continued even before the Sequence had ended, subtly, in the background, as if the Eysen had a heartbeat. Without thinking, Rip picked it up off the chip and rolled it around in his hands, inspecting it closely.

Unsure what he was looking for, Rip looked for buttons, slots, anything that might be concealed on the physical exterior.

It occurred to him that he'd been so concerned with the images inside, that he may have missed something on the outside. After a thorough inspection, which lasted at least thirty minutes, he saw that the pulse was still there. But something far more exciting was coming from within the Eysen. *Sound.*

Rip could distinctly, if not faintly, hear the sound of wind. Even though there were trees blowing inside the Eysen, he went to check the window, even opened it. The San Miguel night was warm, a bit muggy, but very still. He shut the window and returned to the glowing Eysen. It showed millions of trees, a planet-full, moving in the breeze. The wind swept gently through the trees like waves on the ocean. Currents of air swayed in all directions. It was a sea of trees, and Rip, still sensing the Eysen's pulse, wanted to dive through the crystal. Of everything he'd seen inside the Eysen, this was the most desperate he'd been to get inside of it, and he wasn't even sure why.

"What is below those trees?" he whispered alone in the green and blue glow. He recalled the sessions with Gale, when the Eysen had seemed to respond to their questions. *Did that really happen?* he wondered. "Please, show me what is there." He watched the trees ripple and turn in the swirling air, even imagining they were about to part several times, but nothing happened. Trees. Trees.

He didn't know how long he'd been awake. Shadows danced on the wall, the wind noise grew, until lost, and the room became an endless forest. It wasn't a bad feeling, not hopelessness, but he wanted to see what it was. He *needed* to know. The pulse that had begun as the slightest dimming and brightening of the Eysen's glow now had sound too. Between the winds, he could hear the softest heartbeat, matching the rhythm of the pulse.

Then . . . words. He wasn't sure at first. The wind, the pulse's beat, his exhaustion, a billion trees, the glow, they all confused his senses. But he heard something, or at least he thought he did. Rip strained to hear. *My God*, he thought, *if this thing can talk. . .*

Then, he heard it again. "What did you say?" he said out loud.

At that very moment in Phoenix, Arizona, Jaeger adjusted the audio on his control panel. He was already puzzled by the events of the past couple of hours. "Who the hell is he talking to!?" Jaeger shouted to a subordinate.

"No one else is in that house beside Elpate and Dyce. And look, they're still in another room." The man pointed to another monitor in the bank above them. It showed heat signatures of two bodies in one room, and Rip in his room. The Eysen, in spite of its bright display, gave off no heat and was invisible to their monitoring, a fact that fascinated them even more.

"He's talking to himself," the man said.

"Really? You think Ripley Gaines is asking himself to explain what he just said . . . to *himself*?"

"It's odd behavior, but there is no one in that room with him, and he's not on a phone. We've got everything monitored."

"He's talking to the Eysen," Jaeger said.

"Why not? But, asking it questions?"

Jaeger needed answers too. He already had an analyst working on Gaines' earlier statements, "What is below those trees?" and "Please, show me what is there." But now, Gaines wasn't just asking babbling questions, he had said, "What did you say?"

"Damn it, we should have had video in that room by now." Jaeger was more worried than he should have been, but he sensed that something important was happening and he felt blind.

"Tomorrow."

"But tonight won't be happening then," Jaeger said. The man he'd been talking to looked to a female colleague. She returned a serious look, and shrugged with her eyes.

"Do we have any more from our people down there? Why did he open and close his bedroom window? Was it a signal to someone?" she asked.

"Nothing yet," the man said.

Jaeger repeated Rip's question. "Please, show me what is there."

28

Father Jak led them to a poorly lit room near the back of the church that appeared to be a small, windowless office. Gale was surprised at his apparent eagerness to assist them. It was obvious that he knew of Clastier, but, like the historian, was afraid to discuss him. Yet, at the same time, it seemed as if he wanted to help.

The priest knelt and opened a small safe concealed low in the adobe wall. He pulled several aged, folded sheets of paper out, and then studied them for a moment.

"The Lord works in mysterious ways," Father Jak said, looking hard at Gale again before handing her all of the papers.

Her hands trembled as she recognized Clastier's handwriting on the pages. "They're his letters to Padre Romero," she told Larsen.

"Incredible."

Gale looked up from the letters and into Father Jak's eyes. "I don't understand why you agreed to show us these letters if it is forbidden by the Pope?"

"Many things are forbidden by the Pope," Father Jak said, "but good folks still do them." He smiled. "Anyway, you'll understand when you read them."

"Thank you," Gale said.

"There were apparently more, but these are all that survived. Read this one first," he said, touching the middle letter.

While she perused the pages, Larsen and Father Jak made small talk, mostly about the history of the church and the area in general. The first letter was the longest. Its words so stunning she gasped and stopped several times, meeting the priest's eyes. He simply nodded and gave her a knowing smile. Larsen felt a bit left out, and when Gale moved onto the second letter he hoped to read the first, but she clutched them tightly.

Larsen asked about the *Santos* they'd seen as they came through the church. "Yes, as you must know, they are wooden carvings of our saints. Several in our collection date to the 1700s, and many are from the early 1800s, as are the altar screens."

"They're beautiful. I've been on archaeological digs where we were excited to find relics younger than what you have here," Larsen said to the beaming priest.

"No one move!" Nanski said, entering quietly and pointing the gun in a slow, waving motion at each of them.

"Who are you? What do you want?" Father Jak asked.

"Quiet," Nanski snapped. "You, down on the floor." He motioned to Larsen.

Larsen backed slowly toward the corner, looking for a weapon, but he did not get on the floor.

"I'll take those." Nanski snatched the letters from Gale's hands.

She looked at Father Jak, horrified to have lost the letters.

"You, get down!" he demanded, looking back at Larsen.

"Please, take what you want, then leave us," Father Jak pleaded.

"Empty your pack!"

Gale reached to take off the pack and thought of swinging it into his face, but the only thing in there heavy enough to hurt him was the Odeon. If it didn't hit . . .

"Hurry!"

Gale dumped her pack out on the desk. Nanski looked at the Odeon, and then at her. She thought she detected a smile. He shoved the artifact in his pocket, then grabbed the Clastier Papers and the letters to Flora. Luckily, her small journal remained zipped in another of the pack's pockets. Larsen took advantage of Nanski's brief distraction and charged, wielding an onyx bookend.

Larsen was inches from connecting a blow when three bullets ripped into his chest. The pain was searing and intense, but ended quickly. He was dead before his body hit the floor.

Nanski, eyes wide, turned his semiautomatic pistol to Gale, who was already screaming.

Gale couldn't even hear her own cries with the gun's report still ringing in her ears. Just as she was about to jump toward Nanski, Father Jak shoved her onto the floor. Nanski squeezed the trigger, releasing four shots in rapid succession.

Father Jak had purposely placed his body on top of Gale's. Two bullets hit the adobe wall. Father Jak took the other two.

29

Harmer and Kruse heard the first shots and bolted into the church. They were already in the nave for the second burst. Kruse took a chance and fired down the hall. Nanski, who was standing in the doorway, spun around and got off three shots as he ran toward the back door. Fleeing the building he tried to shoot again, but the gun just clicked, empty. He shoved the papers and letters into the waist of his pants and switched magazines while darting around a neighboring house.

Harmer went into the room. Kruse continued to pursue Nanski.

"Gale?" Harmer whispered, pulling the priest's bloody body off of her. "Are you hit?"

"I don't know, I don't know!" Gale screamed, not knowing that all the blood on her chest belonged to Father Jak.

Harmer swiftly lifted Gale's shirt and did quick inspection. "You're fine," she said, pulling Gale up to her feet.

Gale saw Larsen lying in a pool of blood and went to him.

Harmer took one look and shook her head. "He's dead honey. You might check on the preacher."

Gale numbly turned toward the man who had saved her.

"Don't leave this room. I'm going after him," Harmer said,

running into the hall.

"Father Jak," she whispered, kneeling next to him, slowly turning his head.

He tried to smile.

"My God, you're alive?"

"Nine. One. One," he moaned.

Gale found the phone on the desk and called, then returned to him. "Help is on the way," she said, holding his hand. "Thank you for saving my life."

He didn't respond, his eyes closed. She checked that he was still breathing, but was now unconscious.

Gale heard more gunfire behind the church. The 911 dispatch operator would be alerting the police, who might even arrive before the ambulance. She had to get out of there.

"Forgive me," Gale said to Father Jak's unresponsive body. She took one last look at Larsen and fled the room. The front door of the church remained open from when Harmer and Kruse had made their entrance. She peered out, and then sprinted to the SUV.

Gale was shaking so badly it took her several tries to get the key into the ignition. Finally, she sped away. The first mile or two were difficult, her teary eyes trying to focus on the dark roads. Larsen was dead, Father Jak would probably die also. The Clastier Papers, his letters to Flora and Padre Romero, his Odeon . . . all lost! She was hysterical, but the thought of the letters to Padre Romero helped her regain composure. She had to remember what she'd just read. Gale repeated them over and over in her head while she tried to drive at a normal speed.

San Cristobal, Gale repeated to herself. She knew from her last visit that it was north of Taos. A brochure in the motel where she'd stayed with Rip had advertised that the famous writer, D. H. Lawrence, had owned a ranch in San Cristobal that was open for tours. And now she knew from reading Clastier's letters to Padre Romero, that San Cristobal was also the site of his original church. She could make it there.

Kruse lost Nanski in the twilight. He heard Harmer yelling his name and called to her.

"How many?" she asked.

"I'm pretty sure it's just one."

"Vatican?"

"Yeah. We've seen him before."

Both AX agents held their weapons pointed in front of them. Two Hispanic men with rifles came around a corner. "Freeze!" one of them shouted as they all pointed guns at each other.

Kruse looked at Harmer.

"Might have to kill them," she said.

"FBI," Kruse said. "We're in pursuit of an armed suspect. Go back to your homes."

"Like hell you are," one of them said, aiming his rifle.

Without the slightest hesitation, Harmer fired four shots. The bullets hit inches from their feet as the two men dove behind the building.

"Next time, I won't miss!" Harmer yelled. She and Kruse took off toward their car.

They hopped over the low wall surrounding the church and ran out through the front archway.

"Gale's SUV is gone!" Kruse yelled.

"On it," Harmer said, running back to the church building.

A car, coming from the opposite direction, squealed around the corner of a long dirt driveway. Kruse dove out of the way to avoid being hit.

It was Nanski, who slowed on the other side of Kruse and Harmer's car and in a burst of semi-automatic fire shot out two of the tires. He then fishtailed his car onto the two-lane highway.

Harmer came back out. "You okay?"

"Yeah. Inside?"

"No Gale."

"Damn. Our car is toast. Let's find another one before the cops get here."

They jogged up the dirt driveway that Nanski had come down. They had made it only about a hundred yards when headlights fanned over them. Thinking it might be a vehicle they could take, they snuck back down the drive.

Once close enough, they saw Barbeau and another FBI agent get out of the car, their guns drawn.

The agent driving Barbeau had made a wrong turn near the little town of Truchas. His phone had lost signal, and with it the map guidance system. He thought it was a simple route, but the mistake cost them a precious twenty extra minutes. As they pulled up to the Las Trampas Church, they saw the shot-up car and jumped out, weapons drawn.

It didn't take long to find the bloody bodies of Father Jak and Larsen. The priest still had a pulse. Barbeau called it in while the other agent double-checked the area, looking for witnesses. Barbeau walked out into the nave and cursed his luck.

"Damn it!" he yelled, kicking a pew.

Soon, the New Mexico State Police arrived. EMTs were just behind them. They got Father Jak stabilized, and then called in a chopper to airlift him to Albuquerque.

"Is he going to make it?" Barbeau asked a paramedic.

"If he does, it'll be a miracle."

Barbeau told the state police that he wanted a guard with the priest every second, ordering that two officers be put on his hospital room, if he survived long enough to get to one. "Alert me if he wakes."

The agent who'd been driving returned to Barbeau. "Turns out we missed the action by only a few minutes."

Barbeau shook his head. He should have done a million things differently.

30

Kruse and Harmer hid in a stand of trees about a half-mile up the road. For a few minutes after Barbeau had arrived, they debated whether or not to engage the feds and take their vehicle, but common sense prevailed. Figuring the cops, FBI, even Nanski, would all be heading north toward Taos, they'd been making their way south. Once they felt safe enough, Kruse phoned Booker.

"There was an incident," Kruse told his boss.

"Tell me."

"Larsen is dead, Gale is uninjured, but gone and alone." He paused. "She is quite possibly being pursued by a Vatican agent. Our vehicle is shot."

Booker was silent.

"We need a pick-up," Kruse said tentatively.

"I should leave you there."

"Ojo Sarco is our closest town," Kruse said, ignoring Booker's anger.

"Is this beyond you?"

"You know it's impossible to control every situation. You told us not to smother her."

"I'll get back to you," Booker said before hanging up.

"That didn't go very well," Kruse said to Harmer.

"We screwed up," Harmer said. "We should have had the back of the church covered."

"You should have stayed with her in the church."

"She was safe. Protocol said back up my partner."

"Gale is the mission!" Kruse barked. "And I didn't *need* back-up."

"It won't happen again."

"Good. Let's keep moving."

"How did they know we were here? The Vatican and the FBI?" Harmer asked after a few minutes.

"They must be getting their info from the same source. Everyone is after the same thing."

"So where are they all going next?"

"We need to follow Barbeau."

By the time Booker phoned back they were at Ojo Sarco, a tiny farming community about two miles west of Las Trampas. Booker, even angrier than when they last spoke, told them that his helicopter would be there in twenty minutes.

Barbeau got a call from one of the Director's DIRT agents, who told him what he had already surmised. Gale Asher was in New Mexico.

"Turns out that Booker had a team snatch her from an NSA surveillance team outside Flagstaff."

"Booker is a little too brazen for his own good," Barbeau said. "He's got a warrant out for his arrest, the FBI and Interpol are hunting him, but that's not good enough. Now he wants to tangle with the NSA."

"Tangle? They may just terminate him."

"So Booker's people took Asher to New Mexico?"

"We used satellite imagery to track one of those pricey

Augusta Westland helicopters from the location of the skirmish in Flagstaff to Taos."

"Impressive. Do we know where it landed?"

"We just got the address. It's in Taos." The agent hesitated.

"What's the problem?"

"The NSA could be hours ahead of us on this intel."

"And I'm the closest agent?"

"Yes, sir."

"Then I'm on my way." He signaled to the agent acting as his driver, and then jogged over to the senior New Mexico State Police officer at the scene and gave him additional instructions.

Back on the road, Barbeau called his DIRT contact. "I need to speak with the Director, urgently."

"I'll let him know. What should I tell him is the reason for your call?"

"How about I've got a crazed Vatican agent chasing Gale Asher into the night, I'm on my way to a property where Booker Lipton may or may not be, and, if he is there, he may already be the victim of an NSA assassination."

"I'll tell him, but you should try again when you learn something the Director doesn't already know."

Barbeau hung up, his feelings of isolation more intense than ever. He missed Hall, and although he understood that the Director was juggling a hundred flaming daggers in the ever-increasing crisis, his inability to speak with him made Barbeau fear the situation might be hopeless.

In Arizona, Jaeger left the command center to catch some shut-eye in the adjoining sleeping quarters. He had a new book on the tactics of Pancho Villa, the prominent Mexican revolutionary. They would wake him if the NSA assassin hit Booker in the night.

He expected it would take at least a few more days to track and kill Booker, but he felt confident, and although he was frustrated by not being able to see inside Gaines' room yet, the place was surrounded and under every kind of surveillance in existence. He'd be able to see inside soon and get a first-hand look at what progress Gaines was making. In any case, and in spite of Gaines talking to some invisible entity, things were going very well.

31

Rip had fallen asleep trying to hear the whispering voice in the midst of the wind's noise. The Eysen had dimmed, and shut down soon after his eyes closed, but in that place between waking and sleep he still heard the pulse.

A few hours before dawn, he woke to music. After a few groggy moments of wondering why Elpate and Dyce had music on in the middle of the night, he realized that the music was coming from in his room. Inside the Eysen.

It was something between a whispering voice, a Gregorian chant, and a slow, sad, classical violin concerto. Most of all, it was real and all-consuming. Rip broke into tears, unable to think about anything but the music. It beckoned him, and he would gladly surrender to it forever. The beauty of what he heard moved him like the birth of a baby, the death of a loved one, a miracle, the stars themselves.

Tears streamed down his face as he listened to the sound of creation itself.

Then, parting the trees as if they were silk curtains, a man emerged. Rip had seen him before. He knew him from the Eysen and, he realized, from his dreams. It was the Crying Man he and Gale had first seen in Asheville. The Crying Man walked from the trees, closer and closer to the crystal that enclosed the Eysen until his face filled the entire sphere. He stared at Rip. The two of them cried together, and the shared sense of loss and churning emotions took Rip's breath.

"Who are you?" Rip asked.

The music grew louder.

At the NSA's Phoenix command center, a technician pushed a button and an analyst was sent to wake Jaeger.

As soon as Jaeger got there, they replayed the audio. "*Who are you?*"

"Someone is in that room with him!" Jaeger said. "What do we have?"

The technician pointed to the house. Elpate and Dyce were asleep in their rooms. Only one body in Rip's room. "We can't get anything else, the music is too loud." The tech played the song for him.

"Can't we break it apart? Get under the layers and find the conversation?" Jaeger paced. "Damn it, does Gaines know we're listening?"

Another operative spoke up. "Or does the person he's talking to?"

Jaeger had a sinking felling. "Booker. Somehow Booker is communicating with him."

"Why would he ask, 'Who are you?' Gaines knows Booker."

"Where are we with Booker's hit?" Jaeger asked, trying to find some information on which he could rely.

"If he's in Taos, we should have his location isolated by the morning."

"Break that audio down. Tell me who Gaines is talking to. How is he communicating? Where did he get a device?" Jaeger started doing jumping jacks. "Get me caffeine."

Someone ran for green tea mixed with coffee, his preferred beverage for all-nighters.

"Sir, we could move satellites."

Jaeger knew the operative meant that they could request all communication satellites go dark over that part of Mexico. It would allow them to test where Gaines' call was going. The process wouldn't drop the call, it was more like volleying it, allowing them to trace it. The move was advanced, and risky in that it could also disrupt surveillance of other targets and, most importantly, Gaines.

"Call Washington."

32

Gale drove in a trance-like state, unable to recall most of the drive from Las Trampas, and tragically unaware that Nanski had been behind her since she got on Highway 518. He purposely did not get too close or do anything that might arouse her suspicions. He had everything − the artifact, and a pile of Clastier documents. All that was left to do was kill Gale Asher, then he could call Pisano and rejoin the hunt for Ripley Gaines.

He would have done it already, but he was curious as to where she was going. His suspicions said San Cristobal, and so far it looked as if he might be right. He risked getting closer as they drove through Taos on a busy summer Saturday night. Only one car separated them. At the traffic light near Taos Plaza, he even considered walking up to her window and shooting her. He could be gone before anyone realized what had happened, and if they caught him he'd get off, of that he was sure. But the lure of learning just how much she knew and what he might glean by following her to San Cristobal held him back.

Gale, distraught by Larsen's death, which she knew was real this time, and the loss of the priceless papers and Clastier's Odeon brightened briefly when she realized she still had the chip from inside the Odeon in her pants pocket. Feeling the damp blood on her blouse brought her back down.

"His writings were the treasure," she said to herself.

At the old blinking light intersection north of town, she yanked off her blouse and found the only other one she had in her pack. After wiping the blood off with the old one, she pulled the other one on, and then noticed the light had changed. Relieved there was a patient driver behind her, she drove north on Highway 522.

Just south of Arroyo Hondo, she got paranoid. There was only one car behind her, the same one from the intersection, and did she recall seeing it in town too? Hard to say in the dark. She took a sudden left onto county road B007.

Nanski was shocked by her last second, no signal turn, and reflectively yanked his wheel hard to avoid losing her. His car squealed on the pavement and slid on the loose gravel on the shoulder. He narrowly avoided crashing into a cattle guard before righting the vehicle.

"Oh my God!" Gale yelled as the car rumbled in behind her. She stepped on the gas. Her SUV hit a surprise speed bump and she bounced in the seat, losing her grip on the steering wheel. Dust and rocks sprayed as she got the vehicle back on the road.

Nanski saw her hit the speed bump and slowed just in time to avoid bottoming out. It had been an hour since they'd left Las Trampas. *How long had she known?* he wondered.

It didn't matter. She had to die. He floored the accelerator.

His car rammed into the back of hers, jerking Gale forward. At the same time they both hit a second speed bump. Gale's heavier vehicle came down even, and she held on this time. Nanski skidded into another side road. By the time he caught her again, two more speed bumps had been negotiated. On the fifth bump, he tried to use it to his advantage by hitting her bumper just as it bounced. Besides startling her, the move did nothing. Soon, the pavement gave way to gravel and mostly dirt.

Gale's speedometer moved steadily past seventy, leaving

Nanski twenty feet back in a troublesome spray of pebbles, grit, and dust. She looked ahead, saw only blackness beyond her head-lights, and jammed on the brakes. Somehow her vehicle stopped just before the end of the road. A smaller dirt road ran from right to left. Right looked easier to navigate, and she pulled out just before Nanski's car would have impacted. Instead, he over-shot and slammed into a barbed wire fence.

He was lucky and untangled quickly, but she had a lead as the road wound along a sloping edge and two sharp turns. He caught her again as they descended down a steep, narrow road, colliding into her, losing a headlight in the process. They were in the middle of nowhere, no lights in sight. A perfect place to kill her.

Gale suddenly realized they were driving down into the Rio Grande Gorge. "Damn it!" she yelled, sure there would be no way out.

Crunch. He plowed into her again. This time, the terrain aided him and she went left, up a slight bank, and almost rolled. But she came back down and clipped the front of his car hard, knocking him in the other direction. His remaining headlight showed the cliff.

She slowed a bit, and next time he came against her she hit the gas, cut her wheels sharply right, and sideswiped him hard.

Nanski lost control and his car flew over the edge. The single headlight, like a minor's helmet descending into a deep mine, shone into the blackness. It looked bottomless to him. He said a prayer, "I serve the Lord—"

His words went unfinished as the car smashed into the rocky Rio Hondo River, a hundred yards before its confluence with the Rio Grande.

Inside her SUV, crunching on the gravel, the impact had barely been audible, but she'd seen him take the dive. Gale skidded to a stop and jumped shakily from her car. She nearly collapsed, but stumbled to the edge. It was impossible to tell how deep the ravine was, but it was deep. Nanski's car wasn't visible. Gasping, panting, she jerked to look behind her, fearing he might still be there.

Then the flames started. Her relief lasted only a moment as Gale realized that inside the burning car, so far down the cliff, were Clastier's letters to Flora and Padre Romero, as well as the only copy of his Papers not in Vatican hands. The fire grew.

"My God, Clastier's Odeon is down there," she said out loud. If it had been light, she would have tried to climb down. Instead, she cried. "What have I done?"

33

Jaeger studied the green, glowing images of the house in San Miguel de Allende, Mexico, and imagined the glow was coming from the Eysen instead of the night-vision effect. Of course, he wished they had interior cameras already in place, but there were other means of getting what he needed.

"Sir, we have approval from Washington to move satellites," an operative told him.

He could not suppress his delight. "Excellent. Begin it." Jaeger sipped his tea-coffee combo and explored tactics in his mind, grateful not to be bound by laws. The NSA's secret mandate allowed him to do whatever was necessary to protect the nation, and in this case, the Scorch And Burn directive meant he could wipe out the entire village surrounding the house if needed.

Booker might have a ton of money and all the power it afforded, but he was no match for the treasury and the might of the United States. The all-powerful Vatican was also in over its head. Even all the saints of the Catholic Church couldn't help them this time. "Unless God himself comes down to get his hands dirty, and even then . . ." Jaeger smiled.

"Sir." An operative interrupted his thoughts. "There's noise in New Mexico."

"Asher?"

"Possibly. An old Catholic Church in Las Trampas was the site of a shooting earlier this evening." The operative looked at her iPad. "One dead. One critical."

"Shooter?"

"At large."

"ID on the victims?"

"A priest in Albuquerque ICU, named, Józef Augustyniak Kowalkowski."

"That's one person?"

"Yes, sir. The fatality is Larsen Fretwell."

"My, oh, my. Is he *really* dead this time?"

"Multiple bullet wounds. Died at the scene. Confirmation from NMSP."

"And no sign of Asher?"

"No one saw her, but there is something else. The FBI was there within minutes, and the agent in charge, Dixon Barbeau."

"I'll be damned. Get us all over this," he said, turning to another operative. "If Booker and Barbeau are in New Mexico, most likely Asher is too . . . it sure sounds like something messy is going on in the land of enchantment. Either that, or there is one hell of a party about to happen and my feelings are hurt. No one has invited us."

"Yes, sir," the operative said, smiling at his superior's odd way of viewing the disturbing development in the crisis.

"Make sure we crash that party."

Barbeau looked at the map of New Mexico as his driver pushed the speed limit and they raced toward Taos. Everything was marked: blue crosses at Taos Pueblo, San Francisco de Asís, and

Chimayó, a red circle at Grinley's house. He added a cross to San José de Gracia Church and studied San Cristobal.

"She's going there," he said to himself. The agent driving glanced over, trying to decide if a response was expected.

Barbeau felt as if he were chasing ghosts. Larsen dead, alive, and dead again. Gaines was even dead according to the media, and then there were Conway and Clastier.

His phone rang. The Director was in midsentence when he picked it up, but wasn't talking to Barbeau. He was giving orders to people, something about Larsen.

"Dixon, are you there?"

"Yes, sir."

"Keeps getting worse, huh?" Barbeau didn't attempt to respond to the Director's rhetorical question and waited for him to continue. "We tried to keep Larsen's identity quiet, but someone down there exposed it. We even tried the next-of-kin notification rule, but Cable News told us that his kin had already been notified the first time he died! Do you believe this stuff? Now we're fielding about a thousand press inquiries. Who were those brave law enforcement officers trying to apprehend when they died on the hotel catwalk in Atlanta?"

"Next they're going to ask if Gaines is really dead," Barbeau said.

"That's the NSA's quagmire. I still don't know why they went to all that trouble when he was about to leave the country."

"They didn't want anyone looking for him."

"I know that, but we're all still looking, aren't we?" The Director almost sounded amused. "Speaking of which, we just missed Asher, huh?"

"Yeah, I'm working on it."

"Well now you've woken up the entire Eysen-seeking world. A beloved priest in ICU, shot by an unknown assailant. An already dead archaeologist, who happens to be Ripley Gaines' right hand man, gets killed *again*. The media is not going to let this go until they get to the truth."

"What is the truth?" Barbeau asked.

"I was hoping you knew. Call me back when you find it. I have to jump. The President's on another line."

Barbeau didn't get to ask the Director the twenty or thirty questions he had, nor had there been a chance to run his theories and hunches past him. Still, he felt better having heard his voice if for no other reason than to know that he was still alive.

34

Moving satellites, the term for testing and tracking the source, or sources, of originating signals, was rarely done. However, there didn't seem to be a choice in this case. They could not figure out with whom Gaines was talking, and even more problematic was his method of communication.

Jaeger jumped rope while waiting for the results. He knew the NSA had some exposure during the maneuvers, namely the loss of surveillance, but it would just be a few minutes of darkness. Then they'd have an answer.

In a solar-powered bunker located on the same Taos property where he'd met Gale, Booker sucked down a yerba mate power smoothie filled with one of his special blend of herbs. He needed to stay up all night, and this would do it. Two aides assisted him in handling the fast-breaking situations.

"The helicopter is on the way to pick up Kruse and Harmer," an aide began. "More AX agents will arrive in the next thirty minutes. Evacuation plans are in place should the NSA assassin locate you."

"We still have not been able to locate Gale Asher," a second aide said. "The tracking device in her car has been spotty. Our last ping, from near Rio Lucero Road in Taos, showed her heading north. At normal traffic speeds, she could be anywhere in this radius." A map appeared on one of three large screens in front of them.

"Okay. And any luck on the witness in FBI custody?"

"Happening as we speak," the aide responded.

"Good," Booker said. "And the assassin? Do we have an ID? An ETA? Any data?"

The aide shook his head. "Not yet."

Booker picked up his ringing phone. "Incredible! Why would they do that?" he asked the person on the other end. "That's our in, it couldn't be more perfect."

Booker hung up and informed his aides that the NSA was moving satellites, explained what that meant, and told them what he needed them to do.

He set a timer for five minutes, then again immediately worked the phones. One minute, twelve seconds, and two calls later, he reached for his smoothie and pulled up a map of Mexico on another screen.

"Will there be time?" one aide asked.

"It'll be close."

"How long have you known where Gaines was?" the other aide asked.

"We found him about four hours ago. And we've got a BLAX agent in the woods outside the house where's he's hiding."

"Isn't the NSA all over it?"

"They have the house surrounded and satellites monitoring, but we have this tiny window of time."

"Time's a funny thing," one aide said, repeating one of Booker's favorite lines.

"Yes, it is." Booker had long believed that one day he would go up against the NSA or one their affiliated groups. His only advantage would be having more advanced technology than they had. In order to accomplish that, Booker bought any company, patent, or prototype that had anything to do with intelligence gathering or enforcement. He also hired every engineer who showed any promise.

The trick wasn't to give the government any shoddy product, it was to give them the best there was . . . almost. He held back the top one percent of the latest, greatest technology. Once the equipment had progressed further, he'd given them that, and keep the next new best stuff. If the customers weren't satisfied, they would go elsewhere. Booker's aggressive acquisition strategy tried to ensure that there wasn't anywhere else to go, but even that had to be kept secret through elaborate layers of shell companies and countless attorneys shuffling papers. In addition, Booker was unequaled in his ability to buy influence. There was always something someone wanted, or better yet, needed.

All his strategy and preparation left him in an advantageous situation, but it wasn't enough to gain a superior position over the mighty U.S. Government. For that, he used backdoors. Inside each design was a hidden backdoor that could give Booker access to what was being done, used, and collected. They were complex, didn't always work, and usually were not in real time, but it certainly got him closer to being on even footing with the most powerful intelligence agencies on the planet.

Jaeger, breathless, stopped jumping rope and checked his heart rate. "How long until we're back online?" he asked, although he knew it was impossible to know.

"It should be any minute, sir."

"Is there anything yet?"

"No, sir. So far nothing is coming up. We're forty-one percent complete on the second wave-scan and there are no connected devices appearing."

He wiped his face with a towel, checked all the monitors, and motioned for a refill on his tea/coffee. "Get me New Mexico up on those first four screens. I want to know what's going on there. Folks, there are three theatres of war in this thing. Wherever Gaines is, wherever Asher is, and wherever Booker is. Right now, two of our targets are in New Mexico. Taos is a God damned multiplex and I want pictures!"

Outside San Miguel de Allende, Mexico, a single BLAX operative, dressed completely in black, crawled on his belly through the undergrowth. Sixty feet away from him were a pair of NSA agents watching the house, unaware of his presence. Seconds were ticking away. He needed to run, but could only slither. There would be only one shot. Making his mission more difficult were the weapons he carried, along with the critical piece of equipment necessary to complete the assignment.

The BLAX operative knew the NSA's eyes in the sky would be back online in a few minutes. Under his skintight black suit he wore a nylon-mesh embedded with wire that would defeat the thermal sensors, but their technology was capable of some incredible things, such as contour recognition and motion detection. He'd trained in one of Booker's facilities with just such equipment, manufactured by a Booker company.

Booker leaned toward the monitor, as if doing so might bring word sooner. Suddenly, it lit up. "Booker," a voice came over the speaker. "Four seconds to contact, three, two, one. Go."

"Rip?" Booker said. "Can you hear me?"

35

Gale watched Nanski's car, waiting for an explosion. None came. She got lost in the flames, hypnotized by their tragic beauty as if Clastier's words could be absorbed by seeing them burn.

It took a long time for the flames to die. She had no idea how long, at least an hour, and nobody had come. That someone might never occurred to her until she shuffled back to the SUV, and then was surprised that no one had. Even though the road was isolated, it seemed crazy that no one would show.

Turning around would be difficult on the narrow road, but she didn't want to go to San Cristobal tonight anyway. What if there were others after her? For the first time she remembered calling nine one one at the church for Father Jak, so the FBI would be notified. She wondered who the dead man in the burning car was.

Danger and fear clouded her thoughts. She had to get out of there.

Gale drove the rest of the way down the narrow road until she came to a bridge that she recognized. She and Rip had started their raft trip there. Why had she wound up back at this place? She remembered Grinley, another kind stranger like Father Jak. Good, helpful folks who kept getting killed.

Trembling, Gale drove slowly across the John Dunn Bridge, unable to see the dark waters of the Rio Grande. Revving the SUV's engine, she headed up the steep switchbacks on the other side. When she crested the top, the endless mesa greeted her, standing dark. A sea of sagebrush punctured by the occasional distant light, signs of life on an otherwise abandoned section of Earth.

Gale followed the rutted dirt road, not caring where it was going. After a few minutes, she heard a faint clicking. It took her a couple of seconds to realize it was her ring on the steering wheel. She was shaking so much that the SUV was beginning to swerve. Gale had a fleeting thought that it wasn't that cold. She couldn't focus. What was it? Wasn't she supposed to be somewhere? What?

Then the realization came as the SUV left the dusty road and crunched into sage and Chamisa. She was going into shock.

Her head hit the windshield as the SUV took out a juniper before being stopped by a sturdy little cedar. *What do I do?* She opened the door and fell out, woozy. Somehow, in her weakness, she pulled herself up and opened the back door – a jacket, a baseball cap. She got them on and started to jog in place, while rubbing her upper arms.

"Think. Where am I? Taos. Gale. Taos. Gale," she kept repeating. Her teeth were chattering. "Come on! I'm going to die out here after all this?" she shouted into the starry, moonless sky.

She got back into the SUV, cranked the engine, and turned the heat on full blast. Rubbing her arms and stomping her feet, she could feel some improvement. Fifteen minutes later, the engine idled, coughed, and died. Out of gas.

Without thinking about it, Gale got out of the car and started walking toward where she thought Grinley's house had been, thinking it would be a place to hide. Unknowingly, she went in the wrong direction. An hour later, she staggered over a hill and saw an Indian teepee glowing a few hundred feet in the distance. At first, she thought it was a hallucination. Then she remembered where she was. What seems strange anywhere else is normal in Taos.

The glow looked warm and inviting. It didn't really matter if there were a serial killer in there. Gale was about to collapse on the deserted road that could be better described as two foot-trails in the desert. With her remaining energy, she marched through the scrub to the teepee.

"Excuse me," she said, standing a few feet from the flap. "Anyone in there?"

A tall, gangly man emerged, cocking a shotgun. "What the who?" he said gruffly.

Gale thought she was lost in time. The man in front of her was the most authentic looking cowboy she had ever seen. His gray hair fell to his shoulders from under a dirty, white, wide brimmed cowboy hat. A faded red bandana wrapped loosely around his neck, and a worn brown leather vest was tight against his thin frame. He might have been missing a six-shooter strapped to his waist, but he was wearing chaps.

"I'm sorry to bother you, I'm lost, my car . . ." Her knees went.

The man dropped his gun and caught Gale before she hit the dirt. "Cheyenne," the cowboy called. "Help, quick."

A pretty woman appeared from inside. "Who is it?"

"Some tourist or something. Busted car. Gone and fainted."

"I'm not fainted," Gale said sluggishly.

"Get her inside then," Cheyenne said.

Inside was plush and comfortable, not at all what she imagined the inside of a teepee to be. They put her down on the earth floor on top of woven wool Indian blankets and pushed pillows around her. There were several lanterns lit and a small fire in the center.

"I'm sorry. I'm cold." The cowboy put a few more sticks of wood on the fire while Cheyenne covered her with a blanket. "Thank you."

She woke up sometime later and found Cheyenne was sleeping. The cowboy was painting a canvas on an easel.

"I hope you don't mind," he said. "But your face was created
for an artist." He moved a light closer to her. "And your eyes
must have been created *by* an artist."

36

Pisano could not believe someone was pounding on his door at this hour. What time was it anyway? He'd been asleep for hours. Grabbing his Smith & Wesson revolver, he pulled on a robe and walked to the front door of his posh townhouse, just across the Potomac River from Washington, D.C. The gun felt good in his hand. He called it "power in my possession." The Americans weren't any good at fashion, but they made excellent weapons.

Looking through the peephole, he was shocked by the sight of a Catholic cardinal and two stocky Vatican agents.

He put his gun down and hastily undid the locks. The agents pushed their way in as soon as the door opened an inch. Pisano was knocked backwards, but the two agents each grabbed an arm before he hit the floor. They dragged him and deposited him roughly onto a sofa.

"What is your problem?" he said to one of the men. "Do you know how much this robe cost?"

"Quiet," the cardinal commanded. "Do you know who I am?"

Pisano shook his head and gulped hard. He didn't know, but suspected, and it wasn't good.

The cardinal, a man in his seventies with a severe face and a

European accent that was difficult to place, stared. "I am *Exse-quor et Protector Ecclesiae.*"

Pisano had heard of the cardinal known as the "Enforcer and Protector of the Church," but before now he hadn't been sure such a person really existed. It was rumored that he was the most powerful man in the Vatican, more so than the Pope, and even the head of the Vatican Secret Service. Pisano wondered what he had done to warrant a personal visit, and feared he was about to be executed.

"You are not an unintelligent man, Francesco Pisano," the cardinal said, glaring at him. "You love the Church. Your faith is true."

"Thank you, your Excellency. Yes."

"And yet you are an ignorant fool. The *Ater Dies* is upon us, and you sleep here like a baby, like a pampered puppy. You stand when I'm addressing you."

Pisano jumped to his feet. "Your Excellency, please forgive me. If you leave me in charge I will—"

"You are not in charge Pisano! Do you think me a fool?" The cardinal pushed his palm fast toward Pisano's head, stopping less than an inch from his face. Pisano fell back to the sofa, cowering. "There are thousands of you trying to hold back Armageddon."

"Then why are you here?"

"Do not question me. And do not interfere with Joe Nanski. He does not answer to you. It is you who must do his bidding."

"Of course. I understand."

The cardinal shook his head while holding out his hand. Pisano stood and then quickly dropped to his knees. After a short prayer, he kissed the cardinal's ring.

The cardinal motioned for Pisano to rise. Then he walked into the dining room and sat at the table. One of the Vatican agents followed and opened a small laptop computer Pisano had not noticed before.

"Come," the cardinal said.

Pisano joined him at the dining room table and looked at the laptop, where a photo of an Eysen filled the screen.

The cardinal leaned back against the stiff chair as a slide show of images began. "Let me show you why you understand nothing."

37

Rip recognized Booker's voice immediately, but mistakenly thought it was coming from inside the Eysen. He stood, mouth open, staring at the glowing sphere as the Crying Man turned and walked slowly back into the trees as the music faded away.

Distracted, and sad to see the Crying Man leave, Rip wondered how Booker had managed the trick. At the same time, he thought perhaps it was the same method by which the Eysen had been able to show Gale, Sean, and himself in real time when they were at Canyon de Chelly. Baffling.

"Rip, we don't have much time. Please answer me," Booker said.

It felt like being awoken from a dream. "Booker, where are you?"

"At the moment I am in Taos, but that doesn't matter. I've gone to a lot of trouble to tell you that the NSA has your little hide-away there in San Miguel under a surveillance blanket. They can hear everything said in the house. Later today they'll be able to see everything too."

"Why can't they hear you now?"

"They're messing with the satellites and it gave us a brief window – probably less than two minutes left."

"You don't really expect me to believe you after Flagstaff and West Memphis? You were the only one who knew where I was, and yet the FBI showed up both times."

"Rip, they set it up so that you wouldn't trust me."

"Why would they do that?"

"Because I'm the only one who can stop them from taking the Eysen and killing you."

"And they're just letting me have a little Mexican vacation while I try to decode the Eysen? They've got people much smarter than I am who can figure it out."

"Rip, I don't have time to explain, but it has to be you."

"What do you want Booker?"

"For you to be ready. You need to be out of there before the NSA gets the video feed hooked up," Booker said. "By the time you believe me it'll be too late to talk to you, so just listen to me. Keep your pack on your back and the Eysen inside it. My guys will have blue wristbands on that say AX. Be ready to go. Stay on the ground. Life will be a lot easier if you aren't dead."

"I've got a few questions."

An agent broke in on the transmission. "Booker, we are exposed in four."

"Rip, don't say another word," Booker said.

"Two, one, out."

Rip sat in silence next to the Eysen and said nothing. Within a few minutes he was asleep. Hours later the music woke him. It wasn't even music by his definition, and he tried to remember ancient words for music, but even they fell short. One day he hoped to be able to invent an entirely new word for the sounds that emanated from the Eysen.

Violin, cello, or something that sounded like them, a million-voices chant, whispers, a breeze, and a flower blossoming all combined in a soundless universe, supposedly safe to tear down what hardness life had built upon who a person really is at his essence, Rip typed in his laptop, trying to describe what he heard.

Then he stared at the trees, which had filled the interior of the Eysen once again as he waited, anticipating the return of the Crying Man. He was not disappointed as the Crying Man emerged from the forest. This time he used his hands in a slow motion ballet of finger movements to communicate, and, inexplicably, Rip understood.

As the Crying Man squeezed and molded invisible clay in his hands, the story of his people became clearer. It never occurred to Rip that this might be a recorded message. This was the deepest and most meaningful conversation of his life. The intense clarity and absence of any agenda, beyond a desperate need to communicate and be understood, made him feel that his life up until then had been devoid of everything that mattered.

After fifteen minutes of silent talking, and anxious to discover the end of the Cosegans' story, Rip involuntarily asked, "What happened?"

38

Sunday July 23rd

"Pardon my manners, ma'am," the old cowboy said. "My name is Drakeman Ducet." He set his paintbrush down and tipped his hat with a finger, but did not take it off. "Folks call me Drake. Cheyenne, my wife, she calls me all kinds of things, but most of them are sweet." He motioned to the sleeping woman.

"I'm Gale Asher. Sorry to have barged in on you."

"Gale like a storm? It fits," Drake said.

"Some days more than others."

Drake chuckled and resumed his painting.

Gale sat up and looked around. There were dozens of framed paintings leaned against each other. She couldn't see them too well, but most appeared to be western scenes – cowboys on horses, canyons and the like. "You're an artist?"

"I've always tried to be."

She went over to take a closer look at the nearest batch. "They're wonderful." And she meant it. Now curious to see what he was painting of her, she asked, "May I?"

He motioned for her to come behind the easel. "Wow." Although it was unfinished, Gale couldn't believe how well he'd captured her. "My eyes," she said, "it's like looking in a mirror."

"We've all ridden long trails. Only place you can really see it on a person is in their eyes." He considered her face, only inches away, and added a few brush strokes to the painting. "The eyes are formed by all they've seen across every lifetime. Some say each life is a chapter and the eyes contain the entire book."

"Can you read them?" Gale asked.

"Not very well. I'm just an ol' cowboy."

"Don't let him fool you," Cheyenne said, awake now. "That ol' cowboy knows a lot more than he lets on."

"Good morning. Thanks for putting me up," Gale said to Cheyenne. "I'll get out of your way."

"Stay for breakfast," Cheyenne said, "then we'll drive you out to your car and see if we can't get you fixed up."

"Thanks," Gale said, realizing she needed help, but not wanting to bring trouble onto these nice folks. She didn't want anyone else killed. "Is there a place I could . . ."

"If you just need to pee, anywhere out in the sagebrush is fine." Cheyenne pointed to the flap.

Gale excused herself. Outside she found a different world than the one she fell from the night before. There was enough light now to see. Behind the teepee, an old school bus sat deserted, a rusting red pickup truck and a couple of horse trailers kept it company. Beyond that there was a small corral and a shipping container. Gale squatted behind a little juniper tree and tried to decide what to do.

The wind was strong and the sky threatening. Dark clouds loomed, closing in on the mountains and holding back the sunrise. The image of Larsen's bloody, bullet-riddled body lying dead invaded her thoughts.

"Looks like a storm's coming," Gale said as she ducked back inside.

"Morning storms are unusual, but who can say any more about the weather," Cheyenne said. "I better get to breakfast."

Gale was so hungry she would have eaten anything, and was relieved to see Cheyenne preparing a tofu scramble. While they ate, the rains began, blowing hard against the back of the teepee. They opened the front flaps and watched the lightning show.

Drake began work on another painting as the thunder roared and the lightning flashed on the wide-open mesa, silhouetted against the Sangre de Cristo Mountains. "When a storm comes, you got to let it in," Drake said as he danced his brush across the canvas. "You can't keep a storm from coming." The electricity in the air made Gale's skin tingle.

"An out-of-place storm like this brings a message," Cheyenne said.

"Maybe a warning," Gale added.

"Turmoil is usually a good thing," Drake said. A loud thunder boomed, as if on cue.

Cheyenne explained that Drake was a well-known western artist who used to have a busy gallery in Taos and another in Santa Fe, but they gave it all up to live in the teepee. He still sold his paintings, usually for between ten and twenty thousand dollars, but now they enjoyed life. Lightning cracked the sky.

"Do you miss the big time?" Gale asked.

"Not for a minute," Drake said. "I like living without being accountable to nothing and no one, 'cept the sun and the stars, the wind and the rain. We come and go when we like. People let us camp on their land, I give them a painting. We've got places all over the west." Triple lightning bolts hit so close that the ground beneath them shook.

"Sounds wonderful," Gale said, standing to get a closer look at his storm painting, but she froze as two black shadowy figures suddenly appeared, blocking the teepee's opening.

39

They woke Jaeger at six a.m., as ordered. He'd slept for a few hours after moving the satellites, which inexplicably revealed nothing.

"Gaines is losing it," an operative said. "All that trouble and he was only talking to himself."

"Unless there is a way to communicate through that thing undetected," Jaeger said while doing his fifty morning pushups.

"What thing?"

"The Eysen." Jaeger stopped and looked up at the operative, bewildered. "The NSA recruits the best of the best and then makes them better than that. We have the finest technology in the world, and yet you are sitting in this room with me during the most important chapter in our nation's history since the signing in Philadelphia." He furrowed his brow. "What do you think we're doing here?"

"Sir, Gaines just spoke again. He still has that music on, but we are able to get it separated. He asked a question, 'What happened?' The computer filtered the words through a psychological analyzer."

"And?"

"There is a ninety-eight point eighty-four percent likelihood that he's talking to a person, and he expects an answer. According to the computer, he is engaged in a serious conversation with someone."

Jaeger shot a look to the operative who thought Gaines was talking to himself. He stood up. "Screw this. I want cameras in there *now*! And I want the Safety Net ready to go. Everyone in San Miguel on standby."

Operatives scurried to work stations. Two left the room, and a few minutes later four more employees arrived. Safety Net was the name of the operation to pull Gaines out and secure the Eysen. Jaeger was willing to let Gaines have the time to decode the Cosega Sequence, believing it would unlock the secrets of the Eysen, but he wasn't willing to lose the artifact. If there were a chance someone else might be able to communicate with Gaines, they needed to bring him back to the United States and lock him down in a government bunker somewhere.

Jaeger had not been comfortable with the situation from the start. Allowing a suspect to remain at large was counter to all his training and experience, but working at the NSA had a way of changing a person's perspective. Having access to all the world's secrets was a reality-distorting process. Not everything was black or white, and the more important things were unlikely to fit in neat little boxes. "Preconceived notions turn out to be a crash course in stupidity," Jaeger frequently said.

A bone-thin relic of a man rushed in and handed Jaeger a file. The aged man, one of the few analysts who consistently impressed Jaeger, looked at him with watery eyes.

"Frightening," he said quietly, then walked away.

Like most of their operations, the NSA didn't have to investigate the Eysen, they only needed to analyze data that others had. The bulk of information had come from the Vatican, the world's leading authorities on the previously unknown priceless piece of technology. For days, the NSA had been producing reports that Jaeger found increasingly disturbing. At first they wanted the Eysen because of the incredible potential it held to propel the

United States' intelligence, military, and business sectors so far ahead of its rivals that America's dominance in the world would be assured for centuries.

But the report he'd just read changed the priorities in a way he couldn't quite figure out.

Jaeger, needing something to reference, tried to recall a time in history when a similar situation had occurred. There was none. A world devoid of the Catholic Church had existed before, but not for two thousand years, and the report detailed not only how the Vatican would fall, but also how it might possibly take all of Christianity with it.

Jaeger knew that churches weren't just a place to hear Sunday services. They also acted as a stabilizing force in the world. Without the Vatican, a power vacuum would be created that could throw the entire world into chaos.

"Sir, Washington is on the line," an operative said.

"Tell them I'll call them back," Jaeger said, looking at the image of Elpate's house on the screen. "We're going in today. Tell me when we're go-ready, and get me the Vatican on the phone."

40

Rip waited for the Crying Man, who, for the first time, seemed to be at a loss, as if he were trying to create a way to answer Rip's question and describe what happened to the Cosegans. After a few moments, he simply shook his head. The music changed. There was an absence that Rip couldn't place at first. The chanting and whispers were gone, replaced by a hum with something organic about it. Perhaps the sound of a distant earthquake.

The Crying Man stared into Rip's eyes, communicating in this new telepathic language of emotions. Rip thought he understood, "There's nothing left to see." Or perhaps, "There's nothing left to say."

A knock on the bedroom door grabbed Rip's attention. When he turned back to the Eysen, the Crying Man was gone, the trees fading. Rip put the Eysen in his pack, then, remembering what Booker had said, slung it over his shoulder.

Maybe it was an NSA agent, Rip thought, picturing Dyce and Elpate silently killed, adding to the long list of deaths he had caused.

"Rip, it's Elpate. You got a girl in there or something? Let me in, man."

Rip opened the door.

"Dude," Elpate, said looking around in an exaggerated manner. "Is she underage or what?"

"Sorry, I'm just working. I'm paranoid."

"Yeah, that's what happens when you break the law. That's why I'm all legit." Elpate laughed. "Want to buy some pot?" he asked, laughing louder.

"No, but I appreciate your putting me up. I know it's a risk you don't need."

"That's okay brother. We're so far off the beaten path, no one is going to find you. Hell, they would have been here by now. Of course you don't have to worry, no one is going to ever be able to get past the twisty lock on your doorknob." He roared with laughter.

Rip couldn't help but laugh at his own ridiculousness. "Come in," he said to the over-the-hill former drug dealer. After all, it was his house. Dyce and Elpate had put their lives on hold for him and for no other reason than that Rip's dad was a friend of Dyce's and Elpate was a friend of Dyce. If not for them, Rip would be in a federal prison or dead instead of having conversations with an eleven-million-year-old entity.

"So what're you working on back here all secret and hush-hush?"

"An old artifact."

"Dyce told me that much," the old Mexican said. With his short, white ponytail and glassy eyes, he looked like he'd been stoned since the 1960s. "But it's cool if you don't want me to know. If the *federalies* torture me, I'd tell them everything. I'm *un poco* afraid of pain." He winced. "In fact, I'm scared of anything scary."

"The truth is Elpate, I don't exactly know what it is. I need time to figure out what it is."

"Take all the time you need, brother. But you're eating my food, and that's cool, but I, ya know, like to see some gratitude. Nothing much, just a little cash for grass every now and then."

"Sure," Rip said, digging in his pocket and pulling out one of Grinley's hundred dollar bills.

"Oh, you're too kind." Elpate held the bill up to the light and then smiled.

"Actually, I'd like to talk to you and Dyce about something." They found Dyce cooking up bacon and eggs with jalapeño peppers and onions. Rip admitted to himself that the food had been worth the hundred he'd just given Elpate.

At Rip's suggestion, they ate outside. There was a small table on the sunny patio that they moved under a shade tree in the backyard.

"Listen guys," Rip began. "I wish I could stay here forever."

Elpate patted his pocket where he'd stashed the money. "You can."

"But I think it's wiser if I move on."

"No dude, you can have the bread back. It's cool. I don't really need it," Elpate said.

"It's not the cash. I'm happy to pay my way. I just sense something in the wind."

"Rip, it's gotta be pretty risky out there still," Dyce said.

"I know, but sooner or later they'll find me. They always do." Rip thought of the motel in West Memphis, Canyon de Chelly, and Grinley's. "Every time I think I've lost them . . . Anyway, the best chance I have is to keep moving." Rip wasn't sure if he wanted to go with Booker, but needed more time to think about it. "Would you be willing to take me?" he asked, looking at both of them.

"Where?" Dyce asked.

"I don't know yet. Farther south. Do you guys have any ideas?"

"When?" Elpate asked.

"After breakfast?"

41

In the early hours of an already warm summer morning, Senator Monroe strolled a path at Camp David, the President on one side, Attorney General Dover on the other. "Mr. President, I assure you that Booker will be dead before the second summit," Monroe said. He'd been summoned to the presidential retreat once the Attorney General got word of the arrest warrant issued for Booker.

"I don't like you, Monroe," the President said.

The Senator gave him a that's-not-news-to-me look and snapped his fingers as he rolled his right hand off in a dismissive gesture. "Like I care."

"And I'm sure as hell not going to let you use the White House to embarrass the Vice President, and me, by arresting the richest African-American in the world."

"Why would you be embarrassed? Booker Lipton is a criminal," Monroe said.

"Aren't we all?" Dover asked rhetorically.

The President scoffed. "I didn't authorize the assassination of an American citizen."

"Are you stopping it?" Senator Monroe asked.

"You know I can't stop it," the President said. "If the NSA

wants Booker dead, that's his own fault. He's done something to threaten national security."

"The NSA has deemed Booker Lipton an enemy of the state," the Attorney General clarified.

"Semantics," the Senator muttered, stopping and turning to face the two men. "Thanks to our friends in Rome, the FBI has enough evidence to put Booker in prison for the rest of his life, probably longer. He's finished."

"You're underestimating Booker Lipton," the President said. "And I'll not be a party to your stunt."

"I'm sorry if you think I'm doing this to embarrass your Vice President, because the last time I checked he was doing a fairly good job of doing that on his own."

The Attorney General stifled a laugh.

"I don't know about you, Mr. President," the Senator continued, "but *I'm* a patriot."

"Well, Senator, I don't know about you, but *I'm* the President."

"Ha! We're both just counting down the days though, aren't we?" Monroe retorted.

"Gentlemen," Dover said. "Please, let's not make this worse. I think the President has made his position clear, and I will inform the Director of the FBI not to arrest Booker Lipton while he's at the White House."

"Really?" Monroe countered. "The Department of Justice has people working overtime all weekend preparing a ninety-two count indictment against Booker. There's a secret grand jury convening Monday morning. If you don't allow him to be arrested, the media will eat you alive."

"The second Eysen summit is not public. They won't even know he's been to the White House and, as for his arrest, until he's indicted—" The President said.

"Leaks are tough to control in Washington," the Senator interrupted, snapping twice and pointing to a nearby Secret Service agent.

"Listen to me Monroe. I'm a lame duck President, and you do know what that means. It means that even before Booker is indicted, I can pardon him. End of story."

The Senator looked the President directly in the eyes. "Do you really think the NSA is going to let you get away with that?"

"I don't give a damn what the NSA thinks!" the President blasted.

"It's your funeral," Monroe said, turning and starting to walk away.

The President grabbed his shoulder. "Are you making a threat, Monroe? Attorney General Dover, did you just hear Senator Monroe threaten the life of the President of the United States?"

Monroe shook loose. A Secret Service Agent brandished his weapon, while another spoke clipped words into his wrist.

The Senator held up his hands halfway and smiled. "Mr. President, you misunderstood me."

The President snapped *his* fingers and pointed at the Senator's face. "That's what I thought."

"Anyway," the Senator began, "you and I both know that I don't have to make threats."

42

The silhouettes, standing in the opening of the teepee and backlit by a sky exploding with lightning, sent terror through Gale. But it was Cheyenne who screamed as she flung the still-hot iron skillet at them. It bounced off one of the intruders' knees and he let out a groan. Drake was going for his shotgun when the other intruder came down on top of him. The one hit by the skillet barged in and grabbed Gale.

She kicked and punched, but was no match for the fit AX agent. "Damn it Gale, it's Kruse!" he said as she bit his hand. His training almost took over and he was about to snap her neck, but instead, he got her in a bear hug. Harmer, now sitting on Drake, pulled a pistol and backed down Cheyenne, who was wielding a knife.

"Put it down," Harmer said firmly.

"Now!" Kruse added through gritted teeth.

Drake moaned. Cheyenne dropped the knife.

"Let him up! He's an old man!" said Cheyenne, who was probably fifty to Drake's seventy-five.

"Promise to be good?" Harmer asked. "Jeez, Gale, we come in peace."

"You know these apes?" Cheyenne asked.

"I'm afraid so. I'm kind of their prisoner."

"Yeah, we're *sort of* keeping you alive you mean," Harmer said sarcastically.

"You didn't do a very good job with Larsen," Gale shot back.

"Enough!" Kruse said. "These poor people don't need to know any more than they already do. Let's get out of here before you give someone a reason to kill them."

Cheyenne looked at Drake, and then at Gale.

"I'm sorry. Maybe you all should pack up and head to one of your other places for a few weeks."

"It's a mighty muddy day to be travelin' off the mesa," Drake said, finding his hat. "We'll be fine. But, I'd appreciate you all leaving." His stern look turned soft. "Gale, do you want to leave with these two?"

"Yes," she said. "It's the safest for everyone."

"All right. Don't worry about us."

Gale nodded a thank you/sorry/please forgive me look and then turned to Cheyenne. "Please leave this morning."

"Okay," Cheyenne said softly, barely audible over the pounding rain on the teepee. "I understand."

By the time Harmer, Kruse, and Gale reached the Jeep, parked a quarter of a mile away, they were drenched and muddy. Gale didn't say a word. She knew where they were heading. She didn't even care how they had found her, but assumed there had been some kind of tracking device in the SUV.

Riding in the Jeep reminded her of Sean, the kid who had gotten them out of Virginia in his Jeep less than two weeks earlier. She still couldn't believe he was dead. And his brother Josh, he'd been like a brother to her. And now Larsen was dead too. What about Rip? Where was he? Was he even still alive?

Booker left the bunker and returned to the main house as soon as he got word Gale had been found. He stood on the covered section of the deck and watched the storm sweep across the valley. It was only drizzling where he was, but a few miles away the sky appeared to be tearing open. His aide found him.

"Want an update?" she asked.

"The lightning is spectacular," he said.

"Not if you're out there in a teepee," she replied. "Did they really find her in one?"

"Gale Asher is a resourceful woman," Booker mused. "I'm sure it's quite a story, but she is refusing to talk to Kruse or Harmer."

"Everything is ready for her."

"Good. And San Miguel?"

"Another hour and our best BLAX unit will be in position. Is Rip on board?"

"One way or another, BLAX is going to get him out of there. We got lucky that those hotshots at the NSA risked moving satellites. Those chances don't happen by accident. Rip will come to his senses."

The aide met Gale, who was a wet, muddy mess, and led her to a bedroom where several outfits of new clothes in her size were waiting. After a shower, the aide asked if she'd be willing to meet with Booker. "I'd like nothing more," Gale said.

"Excellent, but first, there is someone else you might wish to see," she said, heading down the hall.

Gale's heart skipped, thinking it might be Rip. Then concern took over when she realized it might be Senator Monroe. The aide opened the door, Gale took one look, burst into tears, and ran into Grinley's arms.

"Hey, hey, what's with all the tears?" Grinley asked, hugging her. It had been a few years since he'd felt affection like that.

The feeling of being missed and needed soothed his aggravation at having lost his dog, home, and fortune, such as it was. Although he was a career criminal, truth was all that ultimately mattered to Grinley.

"You're really alive. You saved our lives. They killed your dog. You gave us money. You're *alive!*"

"Take a deep breath."

"Oh, Grinley. They're all dead." Gale couldn't stop crying. "Josh, Sean, Larsen, Topper! And I don't know where Rip is."

"You're safe," he said, holding her.

"No, I'm not. And I lost all the things we were trying to protect. And— "

"You're safe right now. Breathe."

She did. How long had it been since she'd written in her journal? Meditated? How long since she stopped? Gale sat on the bed.

"The world's gone crazy," she finally said.

Grinley laughed. "A long time ago."

The aide knocked on the open door. "Excuse me Gale. Booker was hoping to see you now. There's news of Rip."

43

Elpate and Dyce agreed to help Rip get farther south. Dyce had someone doing minor maintenance on the plane, and it wouldn't be ready for several hours, so they couldn't leave until after lunch.

Rip shut himself back in his room to study the Eysen. Remembering Booker's warning, he was ready to go with everything stuffed in his pack, which was already on his back, still partially unzipped to allow space to shove in the precious artifact.

He watched the Sequence as the sphere floated above the Odeon Chip. For a moment the realization hit him anew. The astonishing object before him was eleven million years old, and incredibly, it contained the entire history of the planet. It was impossible, he knew, yet there it was. The Eysen and all the tragedies it had brought had already changed the world.

I can see it in the swirling Sequence . . . Or rather, I feel it, he thought.

He traveled on a tour of the solar system inside the glowing orb. Again, the visuals, way beyond high definition, made him feel as if he could fall into the Eysen and the universe contained in it. All he needed to do was break the glass, or whatever it was made of, and he would be among the stars. The thought frightened him for a moment, as he wondered if the Eysen could consume him and everything else.

An overlay of dashes and circles that he was used to seeing in the Cosega Sequence imprinted the planets like a date stamp on a photograph, except they moved with the footage, and the language was slowly making more sense to him. He had already worked out the numbers of dots, which were actually tiny circles, and how the rings emanating out from them represented tens, hundreds, thousands, and on and on out to millions and billions. But now he'd seen several arrangements of dashes and circles enough to realize that they represented the sun and the Earth, figuring out the Earth's rotation around the sun represented the key to their numbering system, and that linked back to the language. Everything was based on the circles of nature.

Who were the Cosegans? he wondered. "Come back," he whispered to the Eysen, calling the Crying Man to return. He did not. Only the stars and the circles and dashes filled the sphere. The detail of the planets were so incredible that Rip actually laughed, thinking that if NASA knew about the Eysen, it might hire mercenaries and get into the hunt for the artifact.

The beauty of the solar system captivated him to the point where he could no longer concentrate on the circles and dashes. He wished he could record it, but wanted to be prepared in the event Booker was right. As the scenes moved through space, he remembered Josh Stadler's raising the possibility that the Eysen might be like Roswell, New Mexico, the alleged incident where conspiracy theorists believed that a UFO had crashed-landed in 1947. Gale had later made the point that if it had actually happened, the government would have benefited from the highly developed and complex technology. Many people still believe the government, or the military, had used information gleaned from the wrecked craft, and even alien bodies, to advance everything from medical procedures to space travel, computers, and military technology.

He'd thought a lot about that since those conversations. The NSA and Booker clearly had the incentive to want the Eysen for those reasons. The Vatican's motives were different though in that they saw it as a threat to their existence.

Watching the stars and planets move within the sphere, in what Rip believed to be actual footage, reminded him of something else Josh had said that first day. *"I know that there are hundreds of trillions of stars out there. And to think that only a single little planet orbiting one of those stars can support intelligent life is a silly notion."*

Did the Eysen come from space? Did the Cosegans bring it, or did someone give it to them? Were the Cosegans from somewhere else? Were we? All the philosophical questions made him think of Gale. Sometimes the Eysen reminded him of her eyes. There was so much to discover there. He didn't feel betrayed by her as much as he felt confused. With the benefit of distance, Rip thought he had been unfair to her. It had all happened so fast, but all along her passion had been real, had carried him and made him believe more. He missed her.

The Eysen's glow intensified and brought his attention back. The little replica of himself was now standing in a beam of light above the top of the sphere. With "him" the contents of the Eysen filled the room as if he were in a small planetarium. As Rip walked around to "explore" the new world his room had become, he quickly discovered that even a slight movement affected the view. He could zoom in and out, change the scene, or even pull stars from the sky to inspect them.

"Everything is everything!" Rip said elatedly.

Then, surprisingly, the room went completely dark. He wasn't sure what to do until a pinpoint of light appeared at the center of the black globe. Quickly, as if being rebooted, the Cosega Sequence began to cycle through the familiar visuals, but it ended differently this time. Inside the sphere were galaxies reflecting on, and filling, an otherwise empty pool of clear liquid.

Relative to the glittering space above, it may well have been an ocean, or perhaps all the water in creation.

Rip stared, nearly hypnotized by the beauty, until the surface churned and a single tree emerged. At that moment, the significance of what he would later realize was the symbol of beginning life escaped him. He simply watched in wonder.

Suddenly, the faces he hadn't seen since his first days with the Eysen, returned. They were extraordinary, changed, more alive, and made from the semblance of stars. The expressive human forms conveyed emotions of love, compassion, empathy, trust, and wonder, infusing him with a powerful sense of self that was somehow connected to all. Dozens appeared, fading in and out as if they'd been waiting in line to be seen.

Like the Crying Man, some of their eyes welled with tears, but instead of sadness, they were inviting, even loving, making it impossible for him to avoid smiling. At one point, Rip spontaneously broke into laughter. A second later, it felt as if soft, warm arms were hugging him. The "embrace" lasted until a cold ache he'd never been aware of before, but nonetheless one that had been with him his whole life, was replaced by serenity so complete that he fell to his knees and deeply sobbed. It only lasted a few moments.

These were not merely images. He could feel their feelings and understand their minds. Now his tears turned joyful as the expressions and twinkling eyes taught him that the real meaning of life was to live, and the way to live was to trust and love. So many faces appeared, each expanding and reinforcing the lessons with only glances, but ones that he would never forget.

Although the Eysen was obviously more than something filled with history and information, now he realized it was not a machine at all. What it was exactly might never be known, but no longer was he separate and merely on the outside looking in. He was part of everything the Eysen held.

44

Barbeau woke up in another Taos motel to the sound of rain blowing sideways against his window. He'd slept longer than he'd wanted. The storm clouds had refused to allow the sun to rise, and it put him off by an hour.

He called the hospital in Albuquerque and learned that Father Jak was still unconscious and listed as critical. Three DIRT agents joined him for breakfast at the nearby Michael's Kitchen. The coffee helped bring him back to the current year. The previous day's foray into churches, belonging to prior centuries, had left him feeling displaced.

The agents decided to pursue the only solid lead they had remaining: San Cristobal. It actually wasn't very solid at all. The site of a church long since destroyed, where Clastier, long since dead, may have preached. San Cristobal really was a laughable lead, but even if he didn't turn up some critical antique evidence, it seemed the most likely next stop for Gale Asher.

One of the agents took a call. "The Director wants us to keep an eye out for Nanski, the Vatican agent," he reported. "It seems he didn't check in last night or this morning. The Vatican called the Attorney General, and he threw it down to the Director."

Barbeau didn't like Nanski. He'd been impeding the Bureau from the start. Hall had arrested him, and so had Barbeau. As far as he was concerned, Nanski should still be in custody. It worried him though. He figured Nanski had been the shooter at the San José de Gracia Church, mainly because Booker would have no reason to kill Larsen, whom he'd been hiding since the catwalk collapse in the Atlanta hotel. That means Booker's men might have caught up with Nanski, unless the NSA was killing Vatican agents now.

Jaeger shot a stern look at the confused operative. "Don't worry. I know it's Sunday, but that's a workday for them. There'll be someone answering phones . . . make the call!"

"Who at the Vatican do you want to talk to?" the operative asked.

Jaeger furrowed his brow. "Who do you think?"

"The Pope?" the operative asked in disbelief.

"No," Jaeger said exasperated. "I want to talk to the man in charge." He looked down at his file and gave him the name of the cardinal listed in the report as *Exsequor et Protector Ecclesiae*. *Enforcer and Protector of the Church*, Jaeger thought to himself. *That's quite a title for a man who might just start World War III.*

"Thank you, Cardinal, for taking my call. I wasn't sure you would under the circumstances."

"Yes, well we may be competing for the same thing, but right now Professor Gaines is the greatest enemy of the Church. And, I believe the old saying, 'My enemy's enemy is my friend,' and so must you, or you wouldn't have called," the cardinal replied.

Jaeger appreciated the cardinal's candor and the nod to the old proverb, which had been invoked by several of the great military leaders whom Jaeger had studied.

"I've called you because of a report that just came to my attention. It details the possible collapse of the Catholic Church.

I never imagined such a thing possible, but apparently the Vatican has long feared this disaster." Jaeger paused to give the cardinal a chance to fill in some gaps, or even acknowledge the assessment.

The cardinal remained silent.

"This event has been prophesized by your Saint Malachy, a defrocked priest known as Clastier, and possibly others. Something the Church refers to as *Ater Dies,* Latin for Black Day, brought about by something we call the Eysen."

"The reason for your call?" the cardinal said, sounding bored.

"You can play it cool Cardinal, but my government knows through many means, not the least of which are the actions of the Vatican Secret Service agents, that the hierarchy of the Church is making preparations for the end. The ever increasing erratic and desperate actions of your agents around the globe, and specifically in New Mexico, all indicate that you are losing faith that you'll be able to secure the Eysen."

"Are you going somewhere with this exposition?"

"I'm stating facts. I should also let you know that I am aware of the exact location of the Eysen. At this very moment, more than a hundred Special Ops soldiers surround it. Additionally, we have three dozen operatives en route to Taos."

"Your point . . . ?" the cardinal asked.

"I am concerned about a world without the Catholic Church."

"And well you should be."

"Our analysts have worked computer models all weekend, and there is no good outcome. It seems that after two thousand years, the Vatican has become so entrenched in the affairs of the world that without the oldest seat of power on the planet, certain chaos ensues. The United States is not interested in that kind of destabilization."

"What kind of destabilization *are* you interested in?" the cardinal asked without a hint of humor.

Jaeger, of course, thought of the Middle East, Asia, South

America, but instead said, "The level of turmoil resulting from the fall of the Vatican would be unprecedented."

"We have a will for survival. The Holy Father has faith."

"Good for you, good for the Pope," Jaeger said, annoyed. "I have something else in mind. A proposal I believe you'll be quite interested to hear."

45

Booker handed Gale a mug of herbal tea. "It's okay," he said at her suspicious glance. "The tea is all natural and will only relax you."

"Thank you," she replied.

"You had a rough afternoon. I'm sorry about Larsen."

Gale nodded, sipping the warm tea. He seemed to mean it. She didn't want to think about Larsen again. Her eyes were still red and swollen from her session with Grinley.

"Thank you for freeing Grinley," she said. "I'm sure that wasn't easy."

"I keep my word."

She stared into his eyes, trying to decide whether he was good or bad. After a second she knew the answer. Like most of us, he was both, but Booker dealt in extremes, so he could be extremely good and extremely bad. Gale wanted to ask how he decided which to be at any given time. Did he have a code he lived by? Was there some feeling he got, an inner compass of some sort? The reporter in her had a hundred questions for this mysterious man. She stayed silent.

"How did you avoid the Vatican agent?"

"I killed him," she said coolly.

It was Booker's turn to assess her. "Would you care to elaborate on that?"

She thought of saying nothing and liked the idea of keeping him guessing, but the more he knew, the more he could help . . . if that's what he wanted to do. "His car is at the bottom of a deep ravine that leads to the Rio Grande Gorge, not far from where I abandoned the SUV. He was trying to force me off the road. We traded crashes. I won."

"There have been no reports on the police bands."

"The area is a little remote. I guess with the storm no one has found it yet."

"Are you okay Gale?"

"Someone said you had word of Rip?"

Booker considered pressing her on his question, then decided she was not okay and it was best to leave that alone. There would be time to heal if she survived, and if she didn't survive, her physical and mental health at the moment wouldn't matter.

"Rip is in Mexico. I've talked to him. We have a team there, and they're going to bring him here today."

"How? Where?"

"Even if I could answer those questions, I wouldn't."

"Okay. But he'll be here today?"

"That is the plan. In the meantime, there are some things you need to know about what is going on, but first, I need a favor."

"You still want me to call Monroe."

"Yes. The Senator, if he is in fact 'the empty man who walks among the merchants, the state, and the Church' who will be killed' . . ." Booker said, quoting one of Clastier's five remaining Divinations, "then you need to explain the consequences to him."

"Last time you and I spoke about this we agreed that if Monroe is the empty man Clastier speaks of, then it can only mean that he is the one who winds up with the Eysen."

"Yes, why else would he be killed and his death prophesized?"

"Right, so why is he going to want to give up the Eysen? Monroe is a man seeking power, and I assure you there is nothing more powerful on this planet than possessing the Eysen." She eyed him carefully, knowing her last statement would have an impact on a man who had done so much for untold years to get the very thing of which she spoke.

Booker, aware of her stare, delivered a legendary poker face. "I assume he is not aware of the Divination predicting his death."

"I think not," Gale said.

"He is about to become President, which is not a good time to die. If he wants power, that ought to be plenty."

"Why do you care what happens to Monroe?" Gale asked.

"I don't. I care what happens to the Eysen."

"He won't listen."

"Monroe trusts you and knows you have direct knowledge of the situation," Booker said. "He won't want to risk his death. Why do you say that?"

"Because he must die."

Booker stared blankly at her. Why didn't she think there was even a chance? What did she know? She had looked into the Eysen. She could know anything. She could know *everything*.

"The Senator will die no matter what I say to him, whether he believes me or not. Regardless of what action he takes or does not," Gale said with considerable sadness in her voice.

"Why?"

"Because none of Clastier's Divinations have ever been wrong."

46

Rip stood among the swirling stars as his tour of the solar system expanded to the entire Milky Way galaxy, and then beyond. How had they done this? Could it be possible to travel those distances? Could we achieve some limitless fuel or infinite propulsion system in the future? Did the Eysen contain those secrets? And what others? How incredible it could be to unlock this knowledge, and how dangerous?

The Cosegans had evidently seen so much of the future, and yet could not save their own. *If you could see into the future, would you really want to?* Rip wondered. *Is there a reason we don't know the date of our own death? What about the end of our entire society? The species?* These were the types of questions Gale liked to ask and loved to debate. Rip wanted to know the facts of the past, not the theories of the future, but is it possible that they blended at some point?

The Eysen had a way of changing a person, Rip could feel it happening every time he gazed into the glowing artifact. From the moment it first lit up, it was as if a part of him had also been illuminated. The more he saw within the Eysen, the more insignificant his life seemed, and yet being connected to something as large as the universe gave him a sense of being all-powerful.

With the sensation of flying through space, his entire room seemed endless, filled with the drama of space. The speed of travel defied all laws of physics. If Rip wanted to be closer to some planet or star, he needed only to think it and he'd be there.

His virtual wanderings were cut short by Elpate's voice. "Two minute warning," he said.

Rip shot back to Earth. How had the Cosegans achieved the technology to see so much? The future? The stars? And it wasn't just cloudy images in the mysterious mind of a seer, they had somehow recorded events that had not happened in minute detail. This was too big for Rip to handle alone. He could not uncover the keys to the Eysen's incredible potential while looking over his shoulder and running. If he didn't risk losing the Eysen to Booker, he would likely lose it to someone far worse.

After careful thought and trusting his instincts, Rip decided it was time to trust Booker again.

The first step was to carefully zip the priceless sphere into his pack and wait until Elpate and Dyce were ready to go. On the way to the plane he'd find a phone and call the number Booker had given him in the middle of the night. Then he'd ask Dyce to fly him to a remote spot on the coast where Booker would have a team pick him up.

As soon as Jaeger hung up from his call with the cardinal, known as *Exsequor et Protector Ecclesiae*, he quickly returned the call to his superiors in Washington. The priority of the situation escalated substantially when they told him to "open a full window on 1600."

Surprised, Jaeger immediately transferred an operative whom he didn't think could handle the new stage of their mission. All the operatives in the secure room of the command center had the highest clearance, but Jaeger needed to be more than sure.

After the personnel issue was dealt with, Jaeger went to the control panel that stretched in front of a wall of monitors and plugged his password and the code he'd been given to implement the most unusual order of his career.

"Opening a full window on 1600" meant complete monitoring of the President of the United States. The NSA did this anyway, but as far as Jaeger knew, it had never been made part of a mission before this.

The stakes had increased dramatically, and the look on the faces of the operatives in the room showed shock and strain. Computers and humans would now analyze every word uttered by the President. It would all be tested to determine what bearing they might have on the mission to secure the Eysen. The control room went silent as several screens filled with images of various rooms in the White House, including the Oval Office and the President's private residence. More technicians would be brought in to listen to his conversations.

Once the 1600 window was completely operational, Jaeger gave his superiors an update on Gaines and the efforts to locate and terminate Booker. Seconds after that call ended, an operative signaled him. Jaeger went to the section of monitors and techs covering Mexico.

"Gaines, Elpate, and Dyce had breakfast outside, in the yard."

"That seems odd," Jaeger said. "As if he knows we're listening."

"Then back in his room, Gaines said, 'Please come back,' but he was alone."

"Why would he say that? Who the hell is he talking to?"

"Once again," the tech said, "the computers have it near one hundred percent that Gaines was expecting a reply or some action to be taken as a result of his question."

"Sir," interrupted an operative from across the room, "the

President just asked his Chief of Staff to make a call. Normally he would ask his assistant to do that, not the Chief of Staff."

"Who is he calling?"

"Booker Lipton."

"Damn it!"

"Dyce made a call to inquire about the readiness of his plane," another of the Mexico operatives interrupted.

Jaeger could feel the tipping point. It was upon them. Booker had made a move, or was about to, and Jaeger could lose both Gaines and the Eysen. The experiment was over.

"We are full go. Bring in Gaines," Jaeger said loudly, so that the whole room would hear. "Ready the White Sands safe house. I want to be face-to-face with him in a couple of hours." Jaeger spun to the big screen. "Bring it up. I want to see everything live, second by second. Do it now!"

47

Pisano arrived in Taos. There was a slight lull in the storm, but the landing was still frightening in the small, Vatican-chartered plane. He'd prayed constantly on the flight, not for help finding Nanski or even the Eysen, but just to make it safely back to the ground. Once down, he had to run to the terminal and pick up keys to a waiting rental car. His umbrella was no match for the Taos winds, and he was fairly soaked.

"You call this an airport!?" he blasted the woman behind the counter. "There is mud on my pants!"

"Sorry, sir." She smiled. "Taos is famous for its mud."

Pisano didn't doubt that. It looked like the whole town was made of it. He drove straight to the El Monte Sagrado where he'd be staying. The Vatican had booked him in some minor-league motel that was not acceptable. He'd changed it and didn't mind paying the extra. His God didn't expect poverty, even if the Church accepted it.

In addition to changing his room reservation, he'd made several calls while at Presbyterian Hospital waiting to see Father Jak. At first, the FBI refused to let him in the room, but that was quickly remedied by talking to Attorney General Dover. It helped to have the private numbers of powerful people.

The media was in full throttle, and he had to wade through a crowd of reporters just to get into the hospital. The connection to Gaines had been made. Most reporters still believed the famed archaeologist was dead. However, in light of Larsen's second death, some alternative news sites were questioning the validity of the video purporting to show Gaines being killed. The Catholic priest clinging to life was a good story, and the media was digging to figure out how he fit into the bizarre case.

Unfortunately, Father Jak had still not regained consciousness, so Pisano said a prayer and spoke with the doctor, who was feeling more optimistic, but the next twenty-four hours would be critical. Pisano had gone to the Albuquerque hospital straight from the airport. He would have liked to stay to see if Father Jak pulled through, but instead he had to catch a flight to Taos.

His last call before boarding had been to the cardinal.

"Nanski is an old friend," the cardinal said. "You'd better hope he turns up soon. If not, I'm holding you partially accountable."

"That hardly seems fair. I tried to send him to Mexico."

"You left him without any backup. It was your mistake."

Pisano knew the tone in the cardinal's voice was not leaving any more room for arguing. "Forgive me Cardinal."

"Just be sure you find the Eysen, or even Jesus will not forgive you."

Now in his room at the posh resort in Taos, he changed into fresh clothes and checked the latest TV coverage. As he readied to go to the church in Las Trampas to retrace Nanski's steps, he thought about the rest of what the cardinal had told him.

There was finally a glimmer of hope. The Vatican had agreed to work with the NSA and share the Eysen. When Pisano had begun to question the arrangement, the cardinal shut him up. Pisano realized with horror that even the Vatican's sophisticated anti-eavesdropping tactics were not enough against the NSA. Still, he knew that ultimately the Vatican would never agree to share the Eysen. This was just a ploy, an effort by the cardinal, to buy time.

The plan called for an ally of both the Church and the NSA to act as intermediary. Once the Eysen was secure, it would be turned over to the intermediary and an acceptable plan would be devised in which the NSA and the Vatican could each protect what they needed and also use portions for their own purposes. It would be a powerful position, and both sides quickly agreed on the person for the job. The next President of the United States, Senator Monroe.

48

Most of the windows in the house broke simultaneously in an explosion of glass. A barrage of smoking canisters of tear gas followed. With a wet bandana around his head, Elpate dove into Rip's room and shoved him to the floor. He scooped a pillow off the bed and pushed it to Rip's face.

"Follow me," Elpate said in a muffled voice.

"Where?" Rip said, his words hurt. He was glad Booker had warned him. Everything was in the pack on his back, otherwise escaping with the artifacts would have been impossible.

The familiar living room looked suddenly strange and hostile. They crawled through the fog and sharp shards of glass as fast as they could. The growl of engines and a distant radio static made the surreal environment even more foreign. They reached the windowless garage, where Dyce was already waiting in the driver's seat.

"Hell, man, this is real bad!" he yelled, waving a pistol. "They could be waiting out there with a tank."

Elpate hit a button on the wall and followed Rip into the back seat. Dyce timed it perfectly and squealed out of the garage while the door was still rising, with only an inch to spare. A black military vehicle blocked the end of the driveway with shooters lined behind it. Dyce veered into the yard and floored the gas pedal.

Bullets zinged passed them. Dozens of commandos came from everywhere. Rip spotted quite a few with AX wristbands and realized the NSA and Booker's team might have arrived at the same time.

As the old Honda careened over a row of small hedges, Rip looked back and saw the commandos engaging Booker's mercenaries. As a Hummer appeared from the right, Dyce turned left too sharply and their car slid down an embankment. Although close to rolling, he kept it moving. Another vehicle joined the chase.

Hemmed in by trees and pursued by two vehicles, at least no one was shooting at them. *They aren't going to risk shooting the Eysen*, Rip thought. "They want to take me alive," he said. "That's why they haven't hit us yet."

"Even if you're right, that doesn't mean we've got a free pass. All they need to do is shoot out a tire," Dyce said. "Damn it, we're surrounded by trees!"

There was no choice but to enter the woods. It was a frightening prospect, made worse because they were heading down a steep mountainside. Dyce's piloting skills served them well, weaving through trees like a medieval knight riding a gauntlet. He sideswiped a few saplings, but the Honda took the blows like a stock car. Dyce used the momentum of each impact to compensate his steering in the soft ground.

After a few minutes, the Hummer clipped a large tree and crashed. Soon after, the other vehicle turned sharply, trying to avoid a large rock outcropping, and rolled. The momentary lack of pursuers allowed Dyce to slow down to a safer speed.

It was almost ten minutes of bouncing and swerving before they finally found level terrain. Dyce, dripping sweat, yelled back to Elpate. "Any ideas?"

"I'm not sure where we are, but I think if you head right you'll find more houses."

"Why do we want houses?" Rip asked.

"We need to ditch this car and find another."

"Get me a smoke," Dyce said.

Rip thought it was a crazy time to smoke a joint, but was relieved to see Elpate light a cigarette instead, then reach forward to stick it in Dyce's mouth.

"Thanks," Dyce said, exhaling a bluish cloud. "Damn it Rip, they sent freakin' Navy Seals after you."

"Sorry," Rip said. "I don't want you guys to get killed trying to help me. Maybe you should let me out."

"Screw that," Elpate argued. "It's about friendship and loyalty."

"Damn right," Dyce agreed.

Trees blurred by, and for a second Rip thought they might just escape. These two guys knew what they were doing. Rip imagined this was far from their closest shave, particularly for Elpate.

A huge Blackhawk helicopter dropped down from above. A sniper hanging out the side fired a single round. The bullet hit its target in an instant. At the same time he heard the shot, it obliterated Dyce's head. Rip tried to grab the steering wheel as the Honda veered into a stand of thin trees and slammed to a stop. Terror rained down. Droves of commandos appeared from all sides.

Even before Rip could get his hand on the door handle, it burst open. He and Elpate were yanked from the car, rolled on the ground, patted down, cuffed, and blindfolded. It all happened in mere seconds.

For the first time since its discovery, the Eysen was out of his possession.

49

Booker looked at Gale. "Clastier's Divinations have never been wrong because we never had an Eysen. Don't you think it gives us the power to change?"

"Maybe," Gale said, considering that idea for the first time.

"Because if it doesn't," Booker continued, "the other four Divinations could destroy us."

"I know," Gale said. "Should I call Monroe now?"

Booker wanted to talk to her about the Eysen. There were so many things he needed to know, a thousand questions dying to be asked. What if he never got to hold it?

"Yes," he said. "This phone is secure."

"Are you going to stay?" Gale asked.

"Do you mind?"

"I guess not." Gale assumed he had the ability to listen in to the call anyway.

"Gale, honey, I gotta say I was not expecting your call," Monroe said. "Normally, I don't take my phone into church with me, but these are strange days." He paced in front of the large stone church outside Washington, D.C., shadowed by his security detail. He was genuinely shocked to hear from her.

"They certainly are."

"Where are you? Do you need me to send someone for you?"

"No, thank you. I'm okay at the moment."

"Hmm. You might think so, but actually you're alive at the moment only because of me."

"I must admit, during the past two weeks it has felt like I had a guardian angel watching over me."

"Well, I'm sure not going to take all the credit. God and I have an agreement." He laughed.

"I have something to tell you."

"I certainly hope so."

"Are you familiar with prophecies of Saint Malachy?"

"Of course. I'm a Catholic."

"This whole episode may have been prophesized by Saint Malachy nearly nine hundred years ago."

Monroe scoffed. "But the authenticity of his prophecies are more than a little questionable."

"To some."

"Okay, in what way did he address an archaeologist stealing artifacts from federal lands?"

"Come on, we both know there's more to it than that," she said, disappointed that he was playing games.

"Then tell me, Gale. What is this all about? Why did you really call?"

"Do you want the true story, or do you prefer the lie?"

"Hey, let's not get testy. Gale, we're old friends . . . lovers. We don't need to discuss this on the phone. Let me bring you in. We'll sort this out. Tell me where you are."

"Fine, you don't want to talk about Malachy, what about Clastier?"

"Look Gale, you may think this is some righteous cause you can get behind, a story you can investigate, but this is much more serious than you could possibly know."

"You underestimate me."

"No, honey, I don't. It's just that there are people who want you dead. I've been able to protect you up until now, but the situation is rapidly changing, and even my power has its limits."

"I thought you said you had an agreement with God."

"God is a busy man these days."

"Is it possible that you've read Clastier's Divinations?"

"His what?"

"Clastier also made many prophecies."

"Really? And you've read them?"

"Yes. They have all come true. Five remain. One is about you."

He walked toward his car. "Let me guess. He predicts my presidency and the greatness that I bring as leader of the world?"

"No. It predicts your death."

He remained silent for several seconds. "Do you wish me dead?" he asked angrily.

"Of course not."

"Do you think I have not sinned? Do you think I have not paid a price for all that I have done? You know me better than that."

"I believe you are a good man."

"Then why, Gale, why on the eve of my greatest triumph have you wrought this kind of firestorm onto my doorstep?"

"I have *wrought* nothing. I am trying to save your life."

"From what? The predictions of a fraud? Clastier was nothing but a crazy man. He spent too much time in the wilderness with Indians and—"

"You don't know, do you? My God, I assumed you knew. That the Pope at least would have told you with all this going on."

"Tell me what?"

"Clastier had an Eysen."

Silence. Monroe reached his car, muted his phone, and told an aide to contact the NSA to get an immediate location on this call.

"Are you still there?"

"Gale, tell me where you are."

"I can't"

"How do you know that Clastier had an Eysen?" Gale could hear his fingers snapping through the phone.

"I can't tell you that either, but if you take possession of Rip's Eysen, you will be sealing your fate."

"Rip's Eysen?" he shot back amidst a rattle of snaps. "Your buddy Rip *stole* the Eysen from the citizens of the United States. It certainly doesn't belong to him. You expect me to trust you and believe your warning, yet you won't tell me where you are? How you know Clastier had an Eysen? Be assured that God has long ago sealed my fate and a failed priest cannot undue His will."

"What if God's will is recorded in the Eysen?" she asked, trying on the theory for the first time. "What if it foretells everything that will ever happen? Maybe that's how Clastier knew what he did?"

"Blasphemy! He knew nothing!"

An aide signaled Booker. He, in turn, moved his finger across his neck. Gale got the message and ended the call. As far as she was concerned, it was over anyway.

50

Jaeger watched the capture of Gaines on the large screen and smiled. "It was a little closer than I would have liked," he said to an operative. "The arrival of Booker's little army mercenaries, while not entirely unexpected, made things a bit more costly."

"Booker is more of a threat to our interests than any government of a hostile nation," his operative replied.

"Yes. He is the most dangerous man in the world, and it would be helpful if he were dead by the end of the day," Jaeger said as he was dialing Washington. Then he saw something on the monitors that made him hang up the phone.

Just as the NSA commandos were about to load their prisoners – Gaines and Elpate – into the helicopter, another gunship descended and fired a small missile into the NSA's Blackhawk. The commandos scattered into the trees. Rip was dragged until he scrambled to his feet and ran, unable to see, holding onto one of his captors. Thankfully, someone tore off his blindfold. "Come on Gaines. Keep up or you might get killed," his captor said gruffly. "And my mission is not about you winding up dead."

"Where's my pack?" Gaines pleaded.

"Safe."

As they ran back up the hill, Rip continued trying, unsuccessfully, to spot his pack. He did see Elpate, still blindfolded and being pulled along, chained to a commando. Dozens of the NSA's elite fighters moved away from the burning Blackhawk. Suddenly there was a loud *whoosh*, followed by a massive explosion. The gunship crashed in a shower of burning debris. Flaming shrapnel rained in on Rip and the commandos. The flying metal hit several of them. Rip narrowly missed injury as a small fireball landed inches from him. One of the NSA's men had fired a missile into the BLAX gunship, destroying it.

The woods, burning around them, were engulfed in black smoke. Visibility deteriorated. Rip choked and stumbled until a commando managed to get a gasmask on him. Another one clipped a chain around his waist and pulled Rip like a dog on a leash. The groups moved swiftly through the war zone. Rip could barely keep up.

Objects careened in around them; flashes and booms. The impacts produced red and orange smoke, which mixed with the black, creating an alien world. Somewhere behind, Rip heard cursing and the crackle of a radio, coordinates being reported.

Single gunshots rang out loudly, cutting through the noise. Commandos started falling. The accuracy of the shooters was frightening. Each shot resulted in a man crying out or a thud as another fell dead. "Snipers, snipers!" someone yelled.

Without warning, Rip was jerked downhill, tripping and rolling. The commando he was chained to crashed down with him. His arms, still cuffed behind his back, were already sore, but after the fall he feared one might be broken. Bullets whizzed from every direction. "Come on Gaines! In case you haven't noticed, people are trying to kill you!" the commando yelled.

Rip didn't know whether to thank him or try to escape, but quickly decided as another commando took a bullet less than twenty feet from them. "I'll keep up." He did not know how they could live through the firestorm of flames, smoke, and bullets, nor did he expect he would.

They bolted toward where they'd been heading before Dyce was killed. The forest thinned. Soon, through the trees, houses were visible in the distance. The commandos had taken up positions and were shooting back, trying to cover Rip's route.

Breathlessly, he stumbled after the commando until they broke into a residential neighborhood. Their pace slowed slightly as the commando read a handheld screen displaying a satellite map of the area. They cut over one street and Rip noticed two more commandos coming behind them. One was chained to Elpate, the other appeared to have Rip's pack.

Before he could celebrate, they hit the ground and his commando started firing into a nearby wooden fence. A few shots came from the other side, but one of the commandos with Elpate tossed a grenade. That was the end of the fence, and whoever was behind it.

Two more streets and their destination became clear. A dark blue van, with doors open, was waiting at the end of a dirt driveway. They piled in. Someone came down on top of Rip. The van pulled away and fishtailed onto another street as they got the door closed. Rip managed to untangle himself from the others and to partially sit up.

Anxious to talk to Elpate, ask his captors about his pack, and find out who they were, Rip started to speak. A commando shoved him hard against the metal wall of the van, blindfold him again, and slapped duct tape over his mouth. His protests were met with several hard kicks to his thigh and stomach.

More than an hour later, they stopped and were pushed onto what seemed to be a small corporate jet. Someone belted him into a seat. After a hurried takeoff and steep ascent, the plane leveled off to a low cruising altitude. Although in pain and with no idea where they were headed, Rip was happy that at least no one was shooting at him, and he believed that the Eysen was nearby.

Rip tried to get someone's attention to look at his arm, but all he could do was make muffled noises from under the tape and he was ignored. A couple of hours later, commandos started cussing and yelling. "They're shooting!"

"Don't even think about landing. They will not risk hitting us!" someone barked, presumably at the pilot. Suddenly, the plane lost altitude in two rapid plummets.

Blindfolded, his terror magnified, Rip screamed from behind the duct tape. No one cared. The plane rocked to the side and then leveled off for a few seconds. Then it dropped again. The commandos were all shouting, but Rip couldn't hear anything specific between the confusion and his own panic.

The pilot managed to get the plane into a climb, but within moments it went nose-down again. The small craft gained speed, and soon the descent was out of control as they went hurdling toward the ground.

"Heads between your legs! We're going down, we're going down!" was the last thing Rip heard before the impact.

51

Rip jerked back in his seat at the first impact. The pilot had somehow regained enough control so that the plane hit the ground in a way that was slightly more landing than crashing. Metal crunched and twisted. The plane rolled and came to rest at an awkward angle. Air rushed in through a gaping hole in the fuselage. The moans of men and the smell of jet fuel panicked Rip, still blind and unable to speak. He heard flames and desperately tried to work loose, but couldn't move.

For two full minutes he tried to escape the seatbelt, to scream against the tape, to kick, to do anything. Nothing worked. He heard muffled voices, but he was so disoriented that at one point he thought they might still be flying.

"Fire! Get them out before it blows!" he finally heard clearly.

Rough hands ripped the duct tape off, stinging his lips and cheeks. Almost at the same time, the blindfold came off and he was freed from the seatbelt and handcuffs. His arm was killing him. Before he could get his bearings, someone threw him out the door of the plane. Landing hard on a knee, he twisted and rolled in pain. He tried to look back, but it was a blur. A commando got an arm around him and pulled him away.

"My pack!" he yelled.

"The pack?" the guy dragging him shouted to others.

"Negative."

"Negative."

Boom! The plane exploded. He went down. A shower of metal, glass, and plastic fragments hit them. Rip felt as if he'd jumped into a burning pool of nails.

The ringing in his ears exacerbated the turmoil of the scene. He stood and then fell. They were in a cornfield, nothing was clear. He felt numb. Elpate stumbled toward him.

"Doon, aw woo oh nay?" Elpate asked. Rip couldn't understand. Elpate kept repeating his question until Rip nodded, realized he'd been asking, "Dude, are you okay?"

"Yes. I think."

Elpate handed Rip his backpack. He looked up, shocked. Elpate took a small bow.

Rip peeked in and saw the Eysen, then quickly slung the pack on his back. Elpate pulled out a joint, lit it, took a hit, then passed it to Rip.

Rip was actually going to take it, but then saw Elpate's face. A military-style chopper came toward them. The three commandos who had survived the crash ran to cover, and two, still with guns, fired. The chopper hovered closer. Elpate grabbed Rip. "Come on!"

They ran into the cornfield and kept going until Elpate began choking in a coughing fit. Only when they heard the chopper spray bullets across the area did they drop.

"I think they just wiped out all the commandos!" Elpate said, recovering. "We may be able to get away. Go! Go!"

"Where?" Rip asked, stumbling forward.

"We need wheels." Elpate wheezed. "This is a farm. They must have something that moves."

⬤

When the chopper set down, they were already four hundred

yards into the cornfield. The sounds of yelling and gunfire pushed them onward.

"I guess some of the commandos are still alive," Rip said.

"Maybe. We got lucky," Elpate replied between gasps.

"Let's hope they keep each other busy for a while."

Elpate was falling further behind and Rip slowed so he wouldn't lose him. A few minutes later, they saw a farmer standing in his doorway looking into the direction of the downed helicopter.

"Quick, put your hands up," Elpate said to Rip, as he raised his arms. They approached the man slowly. Elpate started talking in Spanish so fast that Rip couldn't follow. The man nodded and talked back. The conversation went on a couple more minutes. Elpate turned around and said, "You can put your hands down. He's going to rent us his truck."

"What?"

"Give me a thousand dollars. Quick."

Rip counted out ten of Grinley's hundreds and handed them to Elpate. The shooting stopped, causing Rip to freeze. He scanned the area with frantic looks, fearing the commandos or AX mercenaries were closer. Rip never thought he'd be happy to hear gunfire, but when it resumed he felt strangely safe, at least knowing where their pursuers were.

The farmer led them to a rusty green Ford pickup that must have been thirty years old. Elpate traded the cash for the keys and they climbed in. Much to Rip's surprise, the truck started easily. A few minutes later they turned off the farm's lane onto a busy road.

"Where are we going?" Rip asked.

"Don't worry, they're busy searching all those cornfields. We're not far from the border."

"What border?"

"The American border, gringo." Elpate laughed.

"It's the Americans who are after us."

"Got a better idea?"

"Anything is better than that. They'll shoot us as soon as we even try to cross into the U.S. They don't let you just drive through with a wave."

"Listen dude, you may be some kind of archaeological genius, but I'm an old Mexican drug dealer, so I think *I'm* the border expert here."

52

Jaeger watched the screen in helpless disbelief as the plane with Gaines and Elpate on board crashed. Then, amazed when his men and the prisoners emerged from the plane, he, an atheist, wondered if his partnership with the Church was already paying dividends.

As the events turned yet again with the arrival of Booker's men, Jaeger sat in quiet rage while he saw Gaines and Elpate slip into the cornfield.

Booker is an evil son of a bitch, he thought. *Why is he making this so damned hard for me? I'd kill him myself, if I could find the bastard.*

"Sir, it looks like we're down to one agent," an operative reported.

"I can see that!" Jaeger said. "How close is our back up?"

"A DEA unit will be there in twelve minutes."

"How many?"

"Sixteen. Well-armed."

"It'll be close. And if Booker's got more damned mercenaries coming it will be another slaughter. Where does he train these people?"

An operative was about to answer the question, but another shook his head. Now wasn't the time.

"They're in a green, late-70s Ford pickup truck heading toward the border."

"Hmm," Jaeger mused. "Now, it gets interesting."

Booker's aide whispered in his ear. He turned to Gale after she ended the call with Senator Monroe. "You'd better come with me. It's not going well."

Gale followed Booker outside. The wind was still gusty, but the rain had all but ended. "*What's* not going well?" she asked for the third time.

Once inside the bunker, Booker finally answered her. "The mission to rescue Rip."

She'd known that was what he'd meant, but didn't want to admit it. The gadgetry and controls looked to her like something out of NASA. She was amazed, and then she saw the monitor showing Rip being pushed out of the plane.

"Oh my God. Is he okay? Is that happening now?"

"Yes," Booker responded. "It's a live feed. He appears okay for the moment."

"Who are those men?"

"NSA commandos."

"Who is that man giving Rip his pack?"

"He's a former drug dealer, and—"

"Where did that helicopter come from? It's shooting at them!"

"That belongs to me."

"You? But they're shooting at Rip!"

"No, they are being careful. They have orders not to hurt him."

"But anything can happen. Can't you get him out of there?"

"We're trying."

She screamed when Rip and Elpate darted into the cornfield

while Booker's team and the NSA commandos engaged in a fierce firefight.

Then the screen went black.

"Where are they?" Gale demanded.

"Not sure if they found us, or if the satellite had an issue," a tech said.

"They found us," Booker said. "Find a work-around. Get us other data."

"Already on it."

"In the meantime," Booker said, turning back to Gale, "it didn't sound like the call with the senator went very well."

"What about Rip?"

"I've got hundreds of the very best people working to get him safely back to us," Booker said, exasperated. Then he took a deep breath. "All is not lost."

It took a while for Gale to calm down, but eventually they got back to discussing the Monroe situation and another call was planned. "We've got to get the Eysen. To see if there is a way to stop Monroe from getting killed," Booker said.

"Why is it so important to you to save him?"

"Normally I wouldn't give a damn if Monroe lived or died. Politicians like him are cheap and easy to replace. Truth be told, with his Vatican and NSA connections, I'd just as soon he was dead," Booker said, as they stood on the deck, watching the remaining strands of the storm move across the valley. Gale had agreed to leave the bunker only when she'd received assurances from every tech that she'd be informed as soon as there was anything to report.

"Then why?" Gale pressed.

"Don't you see? If we can use the Eysen to change the 'empty man' Divination about Monroe's assassination, then we might be able to change the other four still remaining."

Gale nodded. She'd been too caught up in everything else to even consider the much bigger nightmares that lay ahead if the final four Divinations came to pass.

"You'd better get him out of there alive. The Eysen is almost useless without Rip."

53

Pisano had read the report on the flight to Albuquerque. Clastier's early days preaching were spent at a church in San Cristobal, but as it turned out, there had not been a church there until a century later. Vatican archivists had uncovered long-hidden details about his life.

That first church had actually been a small, one-room farmhouse that had been utilized as a storage building by neighbors after the owner had died. Eventually, it came to be used as a school and meeting hall for the scattered settlements north of Taos, including nearby Arroyo Hondo. At some point, Clastier came to preach there.

In the beginning of his career, he spoke of strict Catholic doctrine. He was a magnetic speaker and influenced most matters in the community. He also rose in importance within the region as word of his sermons and kindness spread. Once he moved on to El Santuario de Chimayó, his first official congregation, he never lost touch with his friends and followers from San Cristobal, Arroyo Hondo, and the surrounding areas.

When the Church made its final push to put Clastier to death and remove all traces of his existence from any official records, representatives were sent to San Cristobal. The old one-room farmhouse was leveled, homes were searched, property seized, and many false stories were spread. Still, loyalties remained, and the last time Clastier was ever seen he was riding on horseback heading toward Arroyo Hondo.

Pisano was glad the rain had stopped, but was annoyed that he had to travel the back roads of one of the most primitive parts of the country to seek clues that had been missed by the people who had held his job a hundred and sixty years earlier.

Pisano was a man of faith. The cardinal had done a good job conveying how much was at stake for the Church and the world. However, Pisano was most worried about his position within the Church. If he succeeded in this impossible mission, he would gain the trust of the inner circle and be rewarded with immeasurable power that, once granted, would not be relinquished. Should he fail, he was going to pay with his life. It hardly seemed fair for one lapse in judgment in an otherwise solid career. He trusted it was all in God's hands.

He had squads of people in Mexico, but Nanski had believed the only hope of beating the NSA to the Eysen was in Taos. Pisano intended to find Nanski and, barring that, unravel the mystery himself.

"Divine Guidance is a powerful thing," he said to himself as his phone rang.

"Nanski is dead," the cardinal said. "His car was forced off the road and burned to the frame at the bottom of a ravine. His body had been thrown clear before the fire, or he might never have been identified."

The cardinal went on to explain that a man walking his dog had spotted the wreckage. He also gave him an address in San Cristobal that he'd given to Nanski the day before.

"Nanski had asked us to research any churches related to Clastier. This was the only one he had not yet been to because it has long been destroyed. It is up to you to finish his work," the cardinal said before ending the call.

Barbeau sat in front, next to the driver, with two additional DIRT agents in the back seat. They turned onto the small road that led to the D.H. Lawrence ranch, but instead veered off toward San Cristobal. He expected Gale either to have been there, to be on her way, or, if things were finally going right, to still be wandering the streets of the tiny village.

His satphone rang with the news of Nanski's death. Barbeau considered for a minute whether they should head over to the crash site.

"It's likely that Gale Asher is the one who ran him off the road, proves she was heading this way. Let the state police secure the site and get some regular FBI over there ASAP," Barbeau told the agent on the other end.

They parked at the tiny post office and waited for something to happen. Barbeau felt foolish staking out a whole town, albeit a small one, but he didn't know what else to do. He figured he was due for a break.

Gale felt the clock ticking. Seeing Rip nearly die had brought the urgency to another level. "I can't stand the waiting and not knowing," she said.

"Use this time to call Monroe again."

"No, I know him too well. He needs to stew a while longer."

"There is nothing new on Rip," Booker told her again.

"I need to go to San Cristobal," Gale said. "That's where I was heading when I ran into the Vatican agent."

"Taos is full of NSA, FBI, and Vatican agents, plus at least one assassin. You aren't going anywhere."

"Am I a prisoner now?"

"No, but Gale, we're talking about your life. What could possibly be so important to risk that?"

"Clastier and the answers."

He stared at her for a long moment, unable to get past the burning blueness of her eyes.

"I need a car," she said.

"Only if Kruse and Harmer ride with you."

"If they're ready to go now, and you make sure they know that I'm in charge."

Gale said goodbye to Grinley. As a precaution, he was being moved to a place Booker owned in Cuba. He'd be gone before she returned.

"I'll see you again," she promised him.

"I'm counting on it. Saving you and Rip might have been the nicest thing I've ever done. I used up all the kindness I saved by being mean all those years. Sure hate to think I wasted it."

"I don't think you have a mean bone in your body," she said, kissing his cheek.

Booker gave her an update on the other man who had saved her life. Father Jak was improving. Although he had regained consciousness, his condition was still guarded, but his doctors were optimistic. As Harmer drove through Taos, Gale sat in the backseat, contemplating reasons why a Catholic priest had so easily thrown himself into a hail of bullets to save her. While at Booker's, she had journaled all that she remembered from Clastier's letters to Padre Romero, and it was there that she found the answer.

54

They'd driven only a few miles when Elpate stopped at a cracker-box house with almost all of its chalky blue aluminum siding missing.

"Why are we stopping?" Rip asked.

"I know this guy. He'll help us."

Rip looked back at the road they'd just left, then up in the air. So far, no one was following. Elpate embraced the man who answered the door and a machinegun-fast conversation in Spanish ensued.

The man started walking across the street. "Come on," Elpate said. Rip looked reluctant. "How long do you think it'll take them to find the farmer and learn we took the pickup?"

"Where are we going?"

"America."

"How?"

"Same way the drugs get in."

They climbed in an old Datsun B210 and raced away. The driver was on the phone the whole time. Rip only caught a few words. Elpate told him someone was going to drive the red pickup around for a while and then return it to the farmer at the end of the day.

Within ten minutes, they were weaving through an industrial section of town, then stopped in front of a large, dingy building which was some kind of assembly plant. Rip followed the man and Elpate as they hurried around the side and entered a smaller building. Inside, a warehouse the size of a school gymnasium was filled with rows of shelves from floor to ceiling of neatly labeled boxes. Two armed men nodded to the driver, but eyed Rip suspiciously.

The driver pulled open a large cardboard box on the bottom shelf. The interior turned out to be framed in wood. There was just enough room to crawl inside and grab the top rung of a ladder leading down into the floor.

"I'll go first," Elpate said.

"Go where?"

"It's a tunnel that goes under the border," Elpate said as if it were obvious. "Don't worry, there are lights."

Rip remembered the last time he went into a tunnel and wasn't sure. "Is it safe? Can we trust this guy?"

The driver scowled, shoved Rip, and said, "Screw you, man!"

Elpate said a bunch of stuff in Spanish and the guy calmed down a little, but still looked angrily at Rip.

"You insulted my friend, who is only helping us."

"I'm sorry," Rip said to the man. "I'm running scared."

The man walked away.

Elpate called after him, but he didn't return.

"Sorry," Rip repeated to Elpate, and mimed offering money to the man from Grinley's dwindling stash.

"He'll get over it. Come on."

Rip didn't see any other choice. Going underground was probably the safest place to be. He went in after Elpate, careful not to step on his head. Someone shut the box above them. Rip could see the promised light dimly lit below. The ladder descended about twenty feet. As he reached the bottom, Rip realized that this was a sophisticated operation, and it had probably been a great risk to allow him in to see it.

The tunnel, about thirty inches wide and almost five feet high, stretched far ahead. Ventilation ducting ran along the ceiling next to a strand of electrical wiring with a bulb about every ten feet. Four-by-six timbers framed the ceiling and walls every five feet, and a narrow rail system ran along the smooth dirt floor.

"Wow," Rip said. "Who built this thing?"

"It doesn't matter. It's here, let's go." Elpate seemed agitated by his question.

Rip knew it was a drug tunnel, and was also likely used to smuggle illegal immigrants into the U.S. as well. Once again, criminals had saved him. He realized for the first time that he might spend the rest of his life as an outlaw, although that life might not be much longer than the tunnel. They were heading back into the country that wanted him dead.

Even with the vents above, the air was heavy and dusty. They didn't talk much along the way, but Elpate told him that someone should be meeting them on the other side as long as his friend had gotten over being offended by Rip. Elpate kept a fast pace, but occasionally slowed to cough or to catch his breath.

The tunnel went much farther than he'd imagined. It was impossible to know the actual length, and he didn't want to ask Elpate, but as they came to the ladder on the other end, he estimated they might have traveled nine hundred feet.

"What now?" Rip asked, sweaty and breathless.

"Up," Elpate said, going first.

The climb down had been hard on Rip's arm, but going up was even more painful. He'd been expecting to emerge in another building. Instead, he came out behind a group of low rocks in the middle of the hot desert.

After they were through, Rip helped Elpate push the dirt back to conceal the hatch, then he gazed to the horizon and asked, "Where's our ride?"

"Don't know," Elpate said.

Rip scanned the desert as far as he could see in every direction, and there wasn't a trace of a vehicle.

55

Gale called Monroe again during the drive. Booker had given her an untraceable scrambled phone, but just to be safe he told her to limit the call to no more than ten minutes.

"Honey, I'm so glad you called back. I'm sorry, I was a little cranky earlier. You know when you tell someone they are going to be killed . . . well, there's really no good way to do that."

"I'm trying to help."

"I know you are, and I called some friends at the Vatican who checked into Clastier's – what did you call them? His Divinations? It seems the records are incomplete. Maybe you could get me a copy of what you have."

"I don't think that will be possible," Gale said. "But you need to believe me. You and I have a lot of history and I'm trying to save your life."

"I do appreciate that sweetheart, but I'm trying to save yours."

"It's more than that. There are other prophecies, and if we can change yours, then maybe we change the others."

"And what are those other prophecies?"

"Let's just say they are apocalyptic in nature."

Monroe was silent. He did know Gale well, and he believed

she was telling the truth. According to the Vatican and the preparations they were making for *Ater Dies*, Clastier was also to be believed. "What do you need me to do?" he asked.

"Call off the NSA and the Vatican."

"You overestimate my power."

She didn't think he'd go for that, but she had to try. "Then make sure that no matter what happens, you do not personally take possession of the Eysen."

"Is it that simple?"

"I wish I knew."

"That shouldn't be a problem, especially since we don't even have the damned thing yet."

"Good. I have to go. I'll call again."

Sitting in the parking lot of the San Crisobal Post Office, Barbeau received a vital piece of information from an FBI agent at the scene of the Nanski crash. He smiled when he got off the phone. "They found an address in Nanski's pocket," he told the DIRT agents. "And guess what? It's in San Cristobal, not far from here."

In less than five minutes Barbeau was standing in a field of sunflowers. There was no building at the address, only an empty lot. However, there were old adobe homes on either side. He chose one, hopped the fence, and knocked on the front door. A heavyset, middle-aged Spanish woman answered. After he flashed his credentials, she made a face and spoke only Spanish. Barbeau called over a DIRT agent, who easily conversed with her. She claimed to know nothing about the field next door.

They thanked her and tried the house on the other side. Their knock was answered by an old man holding a beer. He didn't know anything either, but suggested they talk to the man in the house up on the hill. Barbeau hadn't noticed, but at the end of the lot, mature cottonwoods and oak trees took over the field before the terrain turned steep, and a little adobe house sat atop the hill.

"Been there since the days of old," the man said.

The morning rains had left everything muddy, making the hill especially treacherous. Barbeau slipped twice on the climb. *What the hell was he doing here?* he asked himself as another agent helped him up and said, "Look Barbeau, that's not how you become a DIRT agent."

Barbeau didn't like jokes, especially at his expense.

A friendly man in his seventies answered the door. His thick white hair, bright smile, and infectious laugh after almost every sentence made even Barbeau like the guy. He invited them in and happily talked about the history of the area, said he'd met President Reagan when he came through Albuquerque one time. Barbeau had to work to keep the conversation on the empty field, and eventually the man told him what he knew.

"An old school house was there, but it was completely destroyed by some officials from Spain, or Mexico, I don't know which. Said something about crimes against God. I don't know what it was about, but my grandmother had some books from her grandmother that she said they came out of the schoolhouse. This house has been here almost two hundred years. Looks it too, I'm afraid."

"Do you have them?" Barbeau asked hopefully. "The school books?"

"I took them to an antique shop down in Santa Fe maybe twenty, thirty years ago, to see what they'd give me for them. Turns out they were next to worthless. I sold a few chairs and an old fiddle, but he didn't want the books. They're still in a box around here somewhere. I always meant to donate them to that historical society down in Taos, but never got around to it."

For ten minutes the man rummaged through a cramped attic without enough room to stand, accessible only from a rickety ladder, while Barbeau and the other agents waited.

"Found my old army uniform!" the man yelled down triumphantly at one point.

Barbeau had no idea what the books might hold, but he was more hopeful than he'd been since Hall had been killed.

"Hey, here they are. Can you give me a hand?" He lowered the box.

Barbeau flipped through the titles: Arithmetic, World Geography, readers, a couple of hymnals. Then he found one that seemed out of place, a thin, leather bound book with no markings on the spine. He opened it and discovered it had been written in fine script. After scanning a few pages, he found the name Clastier.

All the other books were just antique textbooks. He asked the man if he could borrow the Clastier book for a federal investigation. It seemed to please the man a great deal to be part of something so important, especially when one of the agents wrote him a receipt and Barbeau gave him his card. Finally, Barbeau had beaten the Vatican agents. He didn't know exactly what he had, but believed it was extremely important.

Gale gave Harmer a description of the place she had read about in Clastier's letters to Flora. There was also another mention of "his sanctuary" in one of the letters to Padre Romero. Gale had a feeling that if they could find the place where Clastier began, there might be a way to unlock the Cosega Sequence and change the final Divinations.

Pisano had a similar idea and was less than a mile away, heading to the same place. Only he had an actual address.

56

After twenty minutes of isolated despair, a cloud of dust that eventually became a Toyota Four-Runner speeding toward them, interrupted the horizon.

"You might want to tip this guy and try not to insult him," Elpate said, finishing a joint he'd been smoking.

The driver looked fourteen. Rip hoped he was at least sixteen. The young Mexican-American spoke English, and smiled when Rip handed him three hundred dollars. Twenty minutes later, he deposited them at a convenience store and Rip gave him another two hundred.

"Decision time dude," Elpate said. "I'm out of moves."

Rip looked to the sky, waiting for black helicopters to burst through the clouds. He had only a few thousand of Grinley's money left. There were three payphones hanging on the front wall of the store, and luckily one still worked. He told the operator it was a collect-call. Once someone answered on the other end, without identifying himself, he quickly gave his location.

"Here they come. Man, you got some important friends." Elpate whistled. "Of course, you need 'em, when you got so many pissed off enemies."

The helicopter landed, two BLAX agents jumped out, ran to Rip and Elpate, guided them back, and helped them into the craft. They were back in the air in eighteen seconds, flew in silence for about fifteen minutes, and then set down behind a busy truck depot. Elpate and Rip were pulled back off the chopper.

"What the hell?" Rip asked, fearing that his trust in Booker might have been a mistake.

"Sorry, sir. Precautions."

Another agent got out of the helicopter. "I'm the chief and this is my mission. Gentleman, my apologies. This will be very unpleasant, and there isn't time to make it any other way." The chief looked gravely at Rip. "Professor Gaines, I'll need your pack."

"No."

"It wasn't a question. Hand it to me now, or it will be taken by force."

Four soldiers trained automatic rifles on him. He handed it over to them.

"Thank you. Now, please strip."

"What?" Rip protested.

"You freaks are a bunch of perverts," Elpate said.

The chief put the contents of the pack on a nearby table and began running some sort of equipment over them.

"Clothes off, now!"

Rip undressed.

Elpate was a little more reluctant.

"Do you need help?" one of them asked him.

Elpate rattled off a stream of profanities in Spanish while he undressed.

"We've got hot foil!" the chief said.

"What?" Rip asked.

"Tracking device in your pack," another answered.

Rip felt stupid. Of course they would track him. How did he not think of that?

"Hot foil in the shoe," an agent called. They all looked at Elpate.

"Man, I didn't know," he pleaded, looking from the agents to Rip.

Rip was stunned. "He didn't know."

"How did they get this in your shoe without you knowing?" The chief asked. "This is not a simple task. It would take someone trained twenty minutes to get this in your heel and then closed up. "You're lying."

"Rip, come on. I saved your life man."

"He did. He's saved my life all day. I'm telling you he didn't know."

The chief shook his head. He waved a wand over Rip's camera. "Hot foil."

Rip's heart sank. He looked at Elpate, who had purchased the camera new at a store in town. It hadn't been out of Rip's sight until they were captured. The commandos might have had time to plant the tracking device in his camera while on the plane. That was possible. But would they have bothered when Rip was already in custody and presumably on his way to somewhere secure? The camera and the shoe together seemed very incriminating.

"Dude, I don't know nothing about that," Elpate said with pleading eyes.

The chief raised his eyebrows, and then shook his head. He handed Rip the memory card. "Going to have to keep the camera."

"Rip, I didn't put that there," Elpate said.

"I know," Rip said, but he wasn't sure.

"Now, you won't like this bit," the chief said, "but bear with me and bend over gentlemen." Rip was spared the anal search, but Elpate got the full treatment. They were each given jumpsuits and flip-flops. The chief handed Rip his remaining cash, the Odeon, the Odeon Chip, and the Eysen, all in a black canvas bag with a drawstring.

"What about my computer and my gun?"

"The gun's empty. Let's not take it. The computer is too risky."

"I *need* it."

The chief shook his head.

Another agent pointed to his watch.

"I have to have that computer," Rip repeated.

The chief expertly took the laptop apart in less than ninety seconds and yanked out the hard drive. "This is the best I can do," he said, handing it to Rip. "We're out of time."

57

"You're not going in the bird. They're watching air traffic too closely where you're going. And now we've got hot foil. We'll be taking this heat and see if we can't take some of the attention with us," the chief said. Another agent slid the remaining contents and the pack into a box with their old clothes and shoes, then loaded it onto the helicopter.

Two agents stayed with them and the chopper lifted off the ground. A minivan pulled up beside them. "This is your ride," an agent said to Rip. He and Elpate stepped forward to get into the vehicle. "Sorry you're in the next one," he said, holding out his arm to bar Elpate from entering the van.

"Why can't he come with me?" Rip asked.

"Safer to split you up," the agent said. "We have to go, now!"

Elpate waved to Rip. "You better go."

Rip grabbed Elpate into a hug, "Thank you, my friend. You sheltered me. You saved me."

"In the beginning, I did it for Dyce." He smiled sadly. "In the end, I did it for you."

The agent pulled Rip. "*Now.*"

"You'll get him home?"

"Don't worry, professor. He'll be taken care of."

Rip did worry. As the van pulled away, he thought about the damage that had been done to Elpate's house, the smoke and broken windows, probably more. Elpate had never once complained. They'd mentioned Dyce once since it happened, down in the tunnel while Rip was silently beating himself up over being the cause of another death.

Elpate broke the silence, as if he could read Rip's mind. "Shame about Dyce," he had said quietly. "He was a good friend."

"And a good man," Rip had added, and that was that.

Two and a half hours later, Rip finally stood face to face with Booker.

"Are you okay?" the billionaire asked.

"I don't know, am I?"

"If you mean are you safe . . . yes, for the moment anyway. If you mean, do I forgive you for doubting me . . . I'd have to say that answer is also yes."

"Actually, what I mean is am I safe with you?"

"So, you're still doubting me." Booker took a deep breath. "Why don't you take a hot shower. Your room is the last one on the left. You'll find fresh clothes and shoes." He motioned to Rip's flip-flops and ill-fitting jumpsuit. "Once you're feeling human again, we'll talk. I think once you hear what I have to say, you'll understand the whole story and be able to answer that question yourself."

Jaeger had followed the great escape from the satellites and drones. They'd watched them switch the truck at the house without siding, and he'd known about the tunnel for several years. So once Gaines and Elpate disappeared into the ware- house, they knew where to expect them to surface. Being plucked by an AX chopper near the convenience store had also not been a complete surprise. In fact, Jaeger had been taking a calculated risk that he could get the Eysen, Gaines, and Booker all at the same time.

Booker Lipton had escalated things to the point where he was the first corporation in history to effectively declare war on the United States of America. And Jaeger intended for the U.S., or at least the NSA, to respond in kind.

AX had been clever in dropping them into a busy trucking depot, no doubt owned by the treasonous tycoon. Dozens of trucks departed in the thirty minutes after they arrived, and so did the helicopter with the tracking devices. Now he'd have to raid the depot and try to track each truck, a nearly impossible task, even for the NSA.

That's okay, Jaeger thought. As usual he had a Plan B.

58

Gale, flanked by Harmer and Kruse, strolled through the field of sunflowers. "This is it," she proclaimed. "Everything fits. The stream, the rocky hill, the road."

She studied the area again, thinking back on all she'd learned of Clastier from his letter and papers. She'd even watched him write some of them in the Eysen. *These houses weren't here back then*, she thought, but the one up on the hill is where Clastier would eat breakfast and practice his sermons every Sunday. After he moved to Chimayo, he'd even stayed there when he came back for visits. She had to see it.

It seemed crazy to hope that after all this time, there might still be a clue waiting, or maybe even an answer to what had happened to Clastier after his disappearance. Yet at every one of his churches there had been some kind of message. She said a silent prayer to Clastier as they started up the hill.

"I'm going to keep an eye on things down here," Kruse said. "We may not be the only ones who know about this place."

Harmer nodded.

"Don't scare anyone," Gale said.

Kruse frowned.

They knocked on the ancient front door of the little adobe.

It looked as if it had been carved a thousand years earlier. Gale tried to wipe some of the mud off of her hiking boots.

"Yes, what is it?" a man asked as he opened the door.

"Sorry to bother you," Gale said smiling, "but by any chance would you happen to know anything about the vacant lot down there? I mean, its history."

"Sure, it's got lots of history. It's actually a hobby of mine."

Gale was elated. "Really! Would you mind talking to me about it?"

"I'd be happy to. Come on in," he said moving to the side. "Tell me, why are you interested?"

"Well, it's kind of a hobby of mine too."

"Really?" the man asked, sounding pleased.

Harmer and Gale entered. "I'm sorry, I didn't introduce myself. I'm Gale,"

"Yes, Gale Asher, I know," the man said as he turned and pointed a semiautomatic pistol at Harmer. "Easy, big girl. Take out your gun slowly. I prefer not to kill you at close range, blood is almost impossible to remove from fabric."

Harmer looked into his eyes and decided in an instant that the man was serious and would happily pull the trigger. She might have fought, but there was backup nearby. It wouldn't take Kruse long to come looking. Better to stay alive as long as possible. Her mission was to protect Gale, and handing over her gun seemed the best way to do that.

"Good girl," Pisano said. "Now both of you sit on the couch. You too old man. Come out here now!"

The friendly man in his seventies was trembling so badly that he could barely walk. "Sorry," he said to Gale and Harmer. "He said he'd kill me, and my cat."

"Shut up cry baby, and sit down," Pisano said.

The old man sat next to Gale.

"Now that everyone is settled, we can get a few things straight," Pisano continued. "The cry baby tells me that the FBI has already been here, and that they took an old book." Pisano held up the receipt and Barbeau's business card. "Not to worry, my boss will make a call to Special Agent Dixon Barbeau's boss and I'll have that book by the end of the day. FBI agents are like my personal errand boys."

For a brief moment, Gale forgot the trouble she was facing. Her excitement at hearing that there had been something connected to Clastier made her smile. She'd been right, and Clastier was still helping them.

"Is something funny Gale? You don't mind if I call you Gale, do you?" Pisano asked.

"Nothing."

"Then wipe that smile off your face, sinner!"

Gale assumed the guy was from the Vatican, and knew she needed to buy time. "Why are you afraid of Clastier?"

"Oh, little girl, I am not afraid of Clastier. My mind is clear. It is the confused minds, like yours, that allow a creature like him to take root and destroy. He is destruction Gale. I do not fear destruction because it is my God who does all the construction."

"Mind if I smoke?" Harmer asked.

"Mind if I shoot?" Pisano asked incredulously. "Gale, let's not waste our time arguing. I'm tired and muddy. This whole state is made of mud!" He brushed his hand down the side of his suit jacket. "Let's finish this up so we can all go home. Do you know where Ripley Gaines is?"

"No."

"What about the *Ater Dies,* uh, what you call the Eysen?"

"No."

"Okay, then. Thanks for your help," Pisano said sarcastically. "I don't believe you. Perhaps if I kill the sweet old man."

"In the middle of a Sunday afternoon?" Harmer asked. "I think the neighbors will call the cops."

"Is that so?" Pisano whined. "Do you know who I am? I have full immunity. I'm untouchable."

"I don't know where they are. I came here looking for the book the FBI took."

Harmer felt the situation slipping.

Pisano pointed the gun two feet from the man's head.

Harmer watched his eyes and his fingers. She knew he was about to pull the trigger and lunged for him. The gun went off. Two shots. Harmer screamed, the old man collapsed on the floor. Gale tried to get up, but Pisano kicked her back into the couch. Harmer rolled onto the floor bleeding. She'd taken both bullets.

"Damn you," Pisano said to her body as she rolled weakly to the side. He then turned the gun to Gale. "Normally I don't do this kind of thing," Pisano said while using a handkerchief to wipe some of Harmer's blood from his jacket cuff. "Do you know what this suit cost?" he hissed. "More than your car."

The old man was too scared to get the shotgun he kept in the closet, but that's all he could think about.

"Okay Gale, are you still intent on lying?"

"I'm *not* lying."

"Tell that to God and see if he believes you."

"No!" the old man shouted, getting shakily to his feet. "You let her go."

Pisano gave the man a nasty look, aimed his gun at him, and was about to shoot when something out the window caught his eye. Before he could focus on what it was, Kruse had fired a perfect head shot. Pisano dropped to the floor, dead.

59

Gale went to Harmer. She was still conscious. "Do you have a phone?" Gale yelled to the old man. He just sat there, unresponsive, with an empty stare and trembling hands. Gale scanned the room and saw a phone mounted on the wall by the kitchen door. By the time she reached it, Kruse was inside and next to her.

"Let me," he said.

"Why?"

"Because you're about to call nine-one-one. I'm calling AX," he said, dialing.

"Harmer is about to die. She needs medical attention!"

"AX is faster. We take care of our own," Kruse said, then spoke GPS coordinates and hung up the phone. He wiped the phone clean, and then put on surgeon gloves. "Who's the old man?"

"It's his house," Gale said, going over to comfort the man.

Kruse went to Harmer. She looked up at him as he cradled her head. "Thanks. I guess you need a new tattoo," she said in a faint voice.

He looked down at the three-bullet heart tattoo and nodded. "AX is on the way. The wounds aren't that bad."

"They always say that to people, just before they die."

"Stop talking. You'll make it." He grabbed a light blanket off the couch and wrapped it around her to staunch the blood. The bullets had entered her chest and upper arm, but he only felt one exit wound.

"Three shots fired. Don't you think someone has called the cops?" Gale asked.

"AX will be here in seventeen minutes. My guess is that the local cops have a slower response time."

Gale got the old man calmed. Kruse drug Pisano's body outside the house. About ten minutes later, Harmer fell unconscious. Then, five minutes later, one of Booker's helicopters landed in the front yard. Two AX agents rushed in with a stretcher and took Harmer. They would fly her to Santa Fe where a surgeon, well-paid by Booker, was waiting.

Kruse and Gale worked their way back to the car and drove away six minutes before a New Mexico State Police cruiser arrived at the old man's house. The old man was confused by everything that had happened and wasn't much help with descriptions or details.

They rode back to Taos mostly in silence as Gale, lost in her thoughts, tried to imagine what was in the book the FBI had taken. Kruse, contemplating his fourth kill, didn't want to talk either. The tattoo on his right wrist, depicting three bullets penetrating a heart, had been designed to accommodate additional bullets, and now another would need to be added.

It wasn't worn as a trophy, but more like a torture. Kruse didn't like killing, he just happened to be good at it. He'd fired many rounds in skirmishes, for cover or to intimidate, but only four times with the intention to take life. Booker would offer him a long vacation. He'd never taken it before, but he might whenever this case ended.

Booker greeted them in the driveway.

"Any word on Harmer?" Kruse asked.

"She went into surgery minutes ago," Booker said. "We won't know anything for a few hours."

Kruse nodded and headed inside.

"We have Rip," Booker announced to Gale's delight.

"Where? Is he okay?"

"Here," Booker said. "He's arrived only ten minutes ago, probably still in the shower. It was a very rough day for him."

"Can I see him?" Gale asked, surprised he was really there.

"Soon," Booker said. "I need to debrief him first, then he's all yours."

Gale wondered what it would be like. She might have been wrong about Booker, and Rip might have been wrong about her. Could they get past their disagreements and put the pieces of Clastier and the Eysen together? There was no choice. The final four Divinations were too serious to ignore any longer.

"How did it go with Monroe?" Booker asked, bringing her back from her wonderings.

"He said he won't take possession of the Eysen."

"Do you believe him?"

"I believe the man . . . the politician, not so much."

"He contacted the Vatican, after your first call."

"How do you know that already?"

Booker gave Gale an are–you-kidding look. "They gave him a good rundown on Clastier's Divinations."

"So the Vatican does have them?"

"Yes. And, of course, the St. Malachy prophecies have many similarities."

"That's why he agreed not to take the Eysen. He's scared."

"The cardinal tried to dismiss his fears, but Monroe is definitely worried more about his own mortality than the Vatican's."

"Doesn't he realize they're one and the same?"

60

Jaeger had four locations where he thought Booker would be found. One was Washington, where there were plenty of operatives. However, the President had cancelled the summit and Booker undoubtedly knew he was going to be indicted in the morning. Montana – Booker owned half the state – was another possibility. Idaho and New Mexico were other remote states the billionaire favored. However, given the importance of the region surrounding Taos to the fugitives Gaines and Asher, he'd been betting heavily on New Mexico.

Jaeger had extra agents, soldiers, and personnel from multiple agencies in all the places where he thought Booker would turn up, but he'd amassed a small army around Taos. Even the commandos who'd survived the siege in San Miguel had transferred.

"Booker has declared war on America. Well, I plan on answering," Jaeger told his superior.

"We've notified the President and key members of Congress as to the events in Mexico. It's truly unprecedented that a private corporation, with its own military, would engage covert operatives. Twenty-eight dead, nineteen wounded."

"He did that in a foreign nation. Let's see if he's ready to do the same thing on U.S. soil."

"The threat must be removed," his superior said. "Do not let the Eysen slip away from us."

"Without Gaines, we can't get full access to the Eysen."

"So you say. I believe we have people who can get inside that thing."

"The Vatican has been trying for centuries," Jaeger said.

His superior was about to say, "they're just a church," but knew better. "Mexico is a mess. The media has been whining all day about the church shooting, so just try to avoid anymore unnecessary body bags."

"Getting Booker will not be without carnage. I assume you've got spin doctors working on the story already?"

"That's under control."

After the call, Jaeger again studied the monitors. High altitude drones were doing grids over northern New Mexico, Montana, Idaho, and Washington, D.C.

"I'm going to find you, Booker, and then all your money won't do you a damned bit of good."

Barbeau didn't speak Spanish. Unfortunately, his prize from the old man's house was not written in English. He recognized a few words besides Clastier, but one of the DIRT agents was fluent. Barbeau made it clear that the book was not going to D.C. and he wanted the agent doing the translating to stay with him. They sat in adjoining rooms at a chain hotel eating take-out and waiting for the next break.

Barbeau already suspected that the book was valuable, but once he got the report of the shooting in San Cristobal it became even more critical. With the senior U.S. Vatican agent dead, the presence of two agents, probably belonging to Booker, and most importantly Gale Asher, meant the little book was something he could use as bait or to trade. What he really hoped to get out of the antique writings though was understanding.

Barbeau had another call with the FBI Director. They were indicting Booker in the morning. The Director told Barbeau enough that the Special Agent was concerned not just about his own life anymore, but about the future of the United States.

"Booker is dangerous, but the NSA is worse," Barbeau said to the DIRT agents once he finished the call.

"The NSA has to do what is necessary," one agent said. "The world is different now. There are threats all over the place. Most are small, unconventional, but lethal cells. Booker's army is a frightening example of how effective these units can be if they're well funded. Terrorism is the new World War III."

"But don't you see the possibility of corruption?" Barbeau asked, surprised a DIRT agent was defending the overreaching NSA.

"Of course I do, that's why I'm DIRT instead of straight FBI. But it's a fine line between safety and freedom. We have to be careful not to harm the very thing that protects us from harm."

Barbeau didn't know if he knew how to do that. "I believe if you keep cutting out corruption and follow the rules, truth will prevail. That's what justice is about, and in the end that's what we work for . . . the truth."

"Follow the rules?" the agent asked. "Is that why you let Gaines go?"

"I let him go because I didn't have the truth yet, and you know, as well as I do, that if I had arrested him he would be dead now. Christ, we couldn't even keep an old drug dealer in custody. Booker's brigade busted Grinley out while we were moving him to another safe house. No one knew where he was and yet Booker found him," Barbeau said, still angry he had never had a chance to question Grinley.

He looked over at the agent typing the translation of Clastier's book into a laptop.

"Anything?" he asked.

"Nothing too important yet, except it's not written by your man Clastier," the agent said.

"Oh no," Barbeau said.

"But it's about him."

61

An aide had given Rip some painkillers for his arm. It wasn't broken; it had just been dislocated and bruised. An AX agent popped it back in, then escorted him to a small study on the top floor where Booker was waiting.

"Would you mind showing it to me?" Booker asked.

Rip, still a little hesitant, knew Booker could force him to give up the Eysen. There was little reason to refuse. But he didn't have to tell him about the Odeon Chip. It was dark now, but there should be enough power remaining even without using the Chip.

He took the Eysen out of the black bag that the BLAX agent had given him at the truck depot. Unfortunately, it remained dark as he handed it to him.

"It's beautiful," Booker said, tracing his fingers over the smooth crystal. "Eleven million years old . . . incredible."

"Wait until you see it light up," Rip said. "Although, it appears we'll have to wait for the morning. It's solar-powered."

Booker hid his disappointment well. "Tell me what you've learned about it." He returned it to Rip, anxious to build trust.

"You wouldn't believe me if I told you," Rip said.

"I think you might be surprised what I can believe."

"It knows everything," Rip whispered. "I mean, it contains all the knowledge, information, and images of the entire history of the world. Not just Earth, but the entire universe, and not just up until that point eleven million years ago when they made it, but up until now and even the future."

Booker knew Rip did not exaggerate. The Eysen was everything, and even more than he had hoped. "It sounds like you were right on the money when you dubbed it the Eysen. It really is like holding all the stars in your hand."

"It's so much more than that. It's like being in any moment in history, or at least watching it in brilliant high-def. I can't begin to know how they did it. It would take ten lifetimes just to explore a fraction of what this can do."

"And the Clastier connection?"

"He had one," Rip said, studying Booker and not receiving the shocked response he expected. "It's how he was able to make his predictions, what he called the Divinations."

"I've read them."

"You have?" Rip was surprised, but went on. "Then you know how detailed they were, and that there are five remaining that aren't too nice."

"Can we change them?"

"I don't know. I've been trying to decode what I call the Cosega Sequence. It's this wildly elaborate series of circles and dashes that overlays the spinning Earth, all kinds of cosmic explosions, and the positions of stars. It's complex, but I'm making progress. I have gigs of notes and film on my laptop, which is now just a hard drive."

"I heard about the tracking devices. We'll get you a new laptop and transfer your data."

"Where is Elpate?"

"We took him back to Mexico," Booker said. "I know he helped you escape."

"My dad's oldest friend was killed."

"I heard. Do you want us to notify your father?"

"No, I'd rather it come from me."

Booker raised an eyebrow. "Rip, it's going to be a long time, if ever, until you're able to see any of your family and friends."

"I know," Rip said quietly.

After a few seconds of silence, Booker spoke. "Tell me about what it shows of the future."

"An amazing world. I saw a future beyond the imagination of our best science fiction writers. Floating cars, towering round buildings, domes, solar-powered everything, peace . . . "

"How do you reconcile that with Clastier's final Divinations?"

"I don't know. Something must happen in between."

"Or we change them," Booker said.

"I've figured out enough of the Sequence to understand their number system, and maybe even some of the Cosegans' language. I've named them that. It's all based on circles, orbits, planets . . . very universal."

"Do you have the Chip?"

Rip should have known the BLAX agents would have reported an inventory of his possessions to Booker. There was no way Booker would know how the Chip was used. No one did.

"Yes."

"May I see it?"

"Sure." Rip dug it out of his pocket and handed it to Booker.

He set it on an empty table in front of them. "Could I see the Eysen again, please?"

Impossible, Rip thought, *how could he know?* He handed it to Booker again.

Booker placed it on the Chip and smiled as the Eysen came to life.

62

Booker stared into the sphere, hardly breathing. Rip watched Booker instead of the Eysen. What he saw reassured him. Rather than a diabolical madman bent on world domination that some might have imagined Booker to be, Rip sat mesmerized by the sight of one of the most powerful men in the world, silently crying. Booker made no attempt to wipe away the tears that slowly streamed down his cheeks. He was unable to divert a single modicum of his attention away from perhaps the only thing that could humble him.

After several minutes, Booker finally spoke. "The Sequence?"

"Yes," Rip answered quietly.

"No wonder they want this."

"Who?" Rip asked.

"Everyone who knows it exists."

"There was another one. The Vatican destroyed it," Rip added.

"They still have it, and another," Booker revealed, never taking his eyes off the glowing orb.

"How do you know?"

"The Vatican is better at keeping secrets than any organization or government in the world," Booker said. "But the NSA

and I are better at finding them than anyone. You see, I discovered early in life that there were ways of getting anything I
wanted. Information is power, but the real power is *secret*
information."

"If they have two Eysens, why do they need this one?"

"They don't have the Chips for the others," Booker said.
"And while an Eysen without its Chip is still amazing, it is more
like watching a trailer to a movie instead of the whole feature."

"How do *you* know?" Rip repeated.

"I've spent years studying Eysens, although they are known as
many things. There is more information available on them than
you might think. The Vatican has worked hard to remove any
mention or trace, but people like Clastier have tried to leave
clues and secret messages about them."

"What else can you tell me?"

"Not much. As long as I have been looking, and with all my
expectations, this is already beyond anything I dreamt."

"So you used me to find this for you?"

"Don't sound so offended. I facilitated your destiny. Tried to
make it as easy for you as possible," Booker said. "As foolishly as
you've behaved the past two weeks, I've managed to keep you
alive. I was never your enemy, Rip. I'm the only one you can
trust completely."

"Why?"

"Because I've known all along that this Eysen was yours."

"Mine?"

"As astonishing as it sounds, you've now seen with your own
eyes that the people you call the 'Cosegans' somehow found a
way to see into the future. You, yourself, said the Eysen knows
everything. The Cosegans knew you would find this Eysen.
Don't you see? They left it for *you*."

Rip shook his head. He couldn't believe it, but he knew it
was true. He'd known ever since he first read Clastier. It had
consumed him. He knew when he first saw it, when he decided
to run. He had no idea how, but he'd always known.

"The Eysen, the Chip, they read your DNA," Booker said. "It's why the Vatican can't get in, and the NSA has tried so hard to keep you alive. They want the power, and only you can deliver it."

"Why me?"

"That, I couldn't tell you."

"But the Vatican tried to kill me."

"No. A rogue, deranged agent tried to kill you," Booker said, watching the Eysen fly into the stars. "They would have killed you, but only if they couldn't capture you. But they intended to kill everyone who has seen it because it predicts their doom. The NSA wants the technology. The Vatican wants to save itself, and after hundreds of years of studying Eysens they couldn't fully access, they know their only hope is you."

"Can't they just use my Chip, like you are right now?"

"Maybe, maybe not. It appears to be working, but are we seeing anything more than what you call the Cosega Sequence?"

Rip looked at the Eysen. "Not yet."

"But our aims aren't so different from those of the Church. They want to rewrite Clastier's Divination on the demise of the Catholic Church. We want to stop the final four Divinations."

"Do we?" Rip asked.

63

"Do we what?" Gale asked, walking into the study. Rip turned and they found each other's eyes. Unspoken apologies exchanged, a longing, a lingering look, and then an embrace filled with the breaths they'd breathed so close to death, the lives they'd seen lost, and the desperate cause they shared. They were both surprised by the intensity of their feelings.

"We have a lot of work to do," Gale said, somewhat awkwardly.

Rip, still tasting the kiss that they did not risk, felt numb. "I have so much to tell you."

"I'm glad we're all friends again," Booker said.

"With all due respect Booker," Gale said. "I think you are using the word 'friend' a little too loosely."

Booker held back a laugh, because he knew she was serious.

"I'm so glad you're okay," Gale said softly to Rip.

"And you," Rip replied.

"Rip was just about to tell me why he thinks we might not want to change the Divinations," Booker said.

Gale looked astounded. For her, Clastier's prophesies had become the most urgent matter that they faced. "Stopping the remaining Divinations would save millions of lives," she said.

"Including Senator Monroe," Booker said.

"Monroe?" Rip spat the word.

"He's the Empty Man," Booker explained.

"Well that's good news," Rip said. "See, not all the remaining prophesies are bad."

"You may not like him," Gale said.

"That's putting it mildly," Rip said.

"Yeah, well, he's the canary in the coalmine. If we can change that one, then we can change the others."

"As I've been trying to say, that may not be the best idea," Rip said. "For one, although I know you care for the man, he's a bastard. Could there be a worse choice for our next President? He's been anointed by a corrupt Pope, is owned by corporations, and his loyalty is to the NSA. Hey, where can I send my contribution check? I won't even bring up his colossal ego. It's no wonder his death was predestined. The Cosegans are trying to *save* us."

"I won't argue with you, but what about the other Divinations?"

"Fine, let's discuss them."

Gale, still wearing her pack, pulled out her journal and read from a page:

1. Empty Man aka Senator Monroe is killed.

2. The Church aka Catholicism crumbles.

3. Global pandemics and super-viruses wipe out vast numbers of the world's population.

4. Climate destabilization (man messing with nature) although he's vague on the amount of destruction.

5. What sounds like World War III.

"Yeah, I can see why you might not want to avoid those things," Gale said sarcastically.

"If you'd seen the future I've seen in the Eysen, you may not be in such a hurry to alter it."

"Rip, look," Booker said, pointing to the Eysen, now lit even brighter and showing the city he'd seen.

"There it is!" Rip said.

"Glorious," Gale murmured.

Booker, overwhelmed by the images, was equally amazed that the Eysen seemed to respond to Rip's reference to the future city. They watched what seemed like a tour in silence for quite some time.

It was Gale who finally spoke. "Rip, I don't think that is a *future* city."

"What is it then?" he asked.

"I think it's where the Cosegans lived."

"You think *that* is eleven million years ago?" Rip asked.

"No harder to believe than this sphere being that old," Gale said.

"I'd have an easier time thinking we're looking at another planet," Booker suggested. "That is possible."

"What if it is? If that's the past and not the future we're looking at, then what do you think about his remaining prophecies?" Gale asked.

Rip thought for a few moments, staring into the Eysen, looking at the circular architecture. Even the flying crafts were adorned with circles and engineered in a similar form.

"Maybe we'd better try to stop the Divinations," he said at last. "But how?"

64

Gale, knowing the next part of the conversation would not be easy, took a deep breath. "I found Clastier's letters to Padre Romero."

"You're amazing," Rip said, smiling. "Where are they?"

"A Vatican agent stole them from me. They were destroyed in a fire when his car crashed over a cliff."

Rip closed his eyes. "Did you at least get a chance to read them?"

"I did, but Rip, there's something else . . . the same Vatican agent killed Larsen."

Rip looked from Gale to Booker. "I do not want to stop that Divination. The Catholic Church can go to hell!"

"I'm sorry Rip," Booker offered.

Gale went on to tell Rip about the book that she missed getting in San Cristobal. "This man beat me to it," she said, holding out the card she'd taken from the old man's house.

"Special Agent Dixon Barbeau," Rip said, reading the card. "The man saved my life and let me go free. Maybe he was just working for the NSA, but he did it."

"The FBI and NSA have not had any cooperation on this case," Booker said. "The FBI Director has been working counter to the Attorney General, the President, and the NSA. He is trying to root out the corruption at the top of our government."

"Is that possible?" Gale asked.

"I'm certainly involved with corruption in government, not just ours, but around the world. But the NSA is a different kind of thing. It's about absolute security for the United States, whatever the cost. Those people believe the Constitution is second to national security. So, the only way to end corruption at that level is to destroy the NSA, and that is not possible without revolution."

"No revolution in the Divinations," Gale said.

"Don't be so sure," Booker said. "World War III could start in any number of ways."

Rip looked into Gale's eyes, reassured to see the blue again. If he'd been destined to find the Eysen, what was her role? How had she stayed alive?

"In his letters to Padre Romero," Gale started, jarring him back, "Clastier mentions the Eysen, which he called the Universal Sphere, or sometimes the Black Sphere. He described it briefly, and told Romero that Church leaders wanted it, but that it could not be allowed to fall into their hands. He went on to say," Gale checked her journal, "that one day someone would come to the San José de Gracia Church in Las Trampas and ask for the letters he'd written. He said that only if they were sent by Flora, were they to turn over the letters."

"What was in the letters?" Rip asked, hopeful.

"There were only three. He mentioned others, but those did not survive. In the missing ones, he wrote in detail about how he had used the Universal Sphere to make his predictions. It seems he wanted to refute the Church's claims that he was consorting with the Devil, so he wrote the truth. In it, he explains that only he could make the sphere go deep enough to be able to see the future."

Rip nodded. "It seems to be the case, and Booker has confirmed that by spying on the Vatican."

"It was set up that way so that the Eysen wouldn't affect events past the lifetime it is in currently."

"Meaning we can't change the future?" Booker asked. "Did someone make this rule for a reason?"

"Not a rule," Gale corrected. "Just the way they made it. Once Rip is dead, the 'deep knowledge,' as Clastier called it, will be inaccessible."

"So, we can change things?"

"I think we can, but that's not my point. There is a way, even if you are dead, and I'm afraid the Vatican knows this." She held up her Chip.

"Jesus! Where did you get that?" Rip asked, double-checking to see that his was still under the Eysen.

"Teresa, the old woman in Chimayó, gave me an Odeon. It was Clastier's."

"So the Vatican could use that to get deep inside the Eysen they took from Clastier?" Booker asked.

"Yes," Gale said. "Here's the bombshell. Clastier's Eysen was found when they were building El Santuario de Chimayó. That means he had it for at least forty years."

Rip looked at Gale.

She nodded, answering his unasked question. "The healing dirt."

"What?" Booker asked.

"El Santuario de Chimayó is world-famous for its healing dirt. It is believed to be sacred. There is a small hole in the floor inside the chapel. Pilgrims come from all over the world to take a handful of the earth. Clastier's Eysen was found in that same hole."

"We need to know what's in that book that Barbeau has," Rip said.

"Why is it so important?" Booker asked. "We have our own Eysen and its Chip."

"Clastier had an Eysen for forty years. He wrote two centuries worth of prophecies that have all come to pass," Rip said. "Can you imagine what forty years of constant study would yield from this thing? Nobody was even after him until the last few years. That means he was free to pursue the Eysen's knowledge without fear. He could save us decades of research."

"Decades we don't have," Gale said.

"I have people who can help," Booker began. "I've spent several billion dollars funding research into a new field called Universe-Quantum-Physics or UQP. As you know, quantum mechanics is concerned with aspects of physics at the nanoscopic level, subatomic particles, the theory of everything, infinite layers, and the like. UQP goes beyond all that."

"What *is* beyond all that?" Gale asked.

"That's what I want to know. Other dimensions, metaphysics, psychic phenomena, time travel . . . everything we can't see with even the most powerful instruments. Where did we come from, why is it all here, what holds everything together, when did it start, when does it end?"

"Wow," Gale said. "And you have people working on this?"

"Some of the brightest minds in the world. In fact, I want you to meet a very special individual named Nathan Ryder."

"Are they getting anywhere?" Rip asked, skeptical.

"There have been many promising developments, and now with the Eysen . . ."

65

Jaeger, acting like the general he always wanted to be, worked two phones at once and shouted commands from his treadmill while watching monitors covering five states, including detailed live streams coming in from Taos. The governor of New Mexico had been informed that hostile encounters with domestic terrorists were imminent. Advanced weapons had been deployed and were continuing to be moved into place.

By morning they would have the grids completed and know the location of Gaines and Booker, assuming he was right about Taos, and the NSA would overwhelm whatever force Booker had amassed. Even if it turned out to be somewhere else, the personnel could be transferred to any of the other locations in three to five hours. Jaeger felt good about Monday. He'd even ordered the indictments against Booker to be held.

"No sense indicting a dead man," he'd told Washington.

Barbeau had been informed of the potential battle in Taos. The Director ordered all forty-one DIRT agents, who weren't already in New Mexico, to get there. Additionally, sixty-six regular FBI agents from nearby states were on their way. Both groups would arrive before midnight.

The translation of the ninety-eight-page book Barbeau had taken from the old man's house in San Crisobal was nearly complete. The DIRT agent doing the work had switched to voice recognition software and simply read the Spanish into the computer, which translated it instantly.

It was filled with philosophical passages attributed to Clastier. There was also something called a Divination, which, after he read it, Barbeau realized was a prediction for the future of the planet. The prophecy mentioned the absence of war, hunger, and disease, among other things. It seemed like a wonderful view of the future, a place he might like to live. But the thing that caught his attention was Clastier's line that there was also no Catholic Church in that future. This could explain the Vatican's intense interest. Was it worth the senior Vatican Agent's death? Maybe.

Barbeau knew from reading the material DIRT had prepared that Vatican hierarchy, in spite of what they preached to the masses, believed in prophecies and the supernatural. They had the largest metaphysical library in the world, performed exorcisms, and proclaimed miracles. They believed it was possible to tap a higher power, to see things, to know.

Still, the book didn't seem that important until he read the two pages titled "Universal Sphere". A pupil of Clastier had written the book, someone he was apparently teaching how to operate something that sounded very similar to the reports he'd seen on Gaines' Eysen. Barbeau couldn't figure out how the artifact got from New Mexico to inside the cliff in Virginia, but these appeared to be instructions. No wonder the Vatican, Booker's men, and Gale Asher were all there looking for it.

Everything Barbeau had read about the Eysen, which had come from the Vatican via DIRT, made him doubt that it was millions of years old. It sounded too advanced even to have been created in the present day. So reading about it in a book, that was nearly one hundred and seventy years old, was jarring. The most powerful religion, government, and billionaire in the world were fighting over something from the past that could control the future, and Barbeau had what might be the key to it all.

For the first time since the case had begun, he was terrified. Not for his own life, that was worth about eighty bucks to him. Barbeau feared for all the other people alive and the ones still to come.

"Put the translation on a flash drive," Barbeau told the DIRT agent.

"Done," he said, handing him the drive.

"Thank you. Now delete it off your laptop."

"Delete?"

"I mean so it can *never* be recovered."

The agent nodded. "I'll have to backup my other data, then wipe the drive, but if you're worried about the NSA or Booker, even using DOD protocols won't make it completely secure. People they employ might still be able to get something."

Barbeau zipped the printout he'd been reading and the original book into a nylon evidence bag, then put the thumb drive in his pocket. "Then back up your other data and physically destroy that hard drive. Run it over, pump five bullets into it, whatever. Make sure it can never be recovered. And do it now."

66

Booker had been called away, but came storming back into the study. "It isn't safe to stay here." He looked at Rip. "Elpate was working with the NSA all along. *He* planted those tracking devices."

"Are you sure?" Rip asked, already knowing the answer.

"Damndest thing," Booker said. "Elpate had been laundering money and doing dirty work for the CIA for decades as part of some deal that kept him from spending the rest of his life in prison. He'd been a big kingpin when he got busted by the DEA. His connections were so valuable the feds decided to put him back on the street. Ever since, he's been doing small-time stuff, and they've been looking the other way in exchange for his informing. It was a fluke that you dropped into his lap. The NSA must have felt like they won the lottery."

"He saved my life," Rip said.

"Maybe. It may have just looked that way. We'll never know. Elpate is dead."

"You had him killed?"

"It wasn't me. The Vatican did it. He'd seen the Eysen," Booker paused. "They also have a hit ordered on Grinley. They already killed his two buddies."

"Who?" Gale asked.

"A trucker named Fischer and some other guy, I don't remember his name. I think you drove his truck to Taos."

"Tuke," Gale said sadly. "They killed Fischer and Tuke, and their only crime was helping us. They never even knew the Eysen existed."

"Grinley is safe?" Rip asked.

"Booker sent him to Cuba, even compensated him for his losses," Gale said.

"I'm sorry about all this, but we must leave Taos," Booker repeated. "They are preparing for war, and I plan for us all to be far away from New Mexico before it starts."

"We have to go back to Teresa's," Gale said.

"Why?" Rip asked.

"Because she has the only remaining copies of Clastier's Papers and his letters to Flora."

"Asheville?" Rip asked.

"The Vatican took the place apart," Booker said. "The night you left, a crew moved in and trashed everything until they found them," Booker said.

"The others were destroyed when the Vatican's agent car burned," Gale said.

"We're ready," an aide interrupted. "All sensitive data is loaded in the helicopter."

"Booker, we have to get those papers," Rip said. "Not just to preserve Clastier's work, but because we still need answers."

"The NSA, FBI, and the Vatican are about to detonate northern New Mexico," Booker said. "I don't think you understand that this is not like the other times. It's as if all the agents of evil had to be summoned here to destroy you."

"You're being overly dramatic," Rip said.

"I'm trying to make a point."

"You made my point," Rip said. "All those forces are converging here because as Gale told me forever ago, this is where it all began. This is Clastier's world. They're after him as much as us, and if we don't save his work then we're all lost . . . All of us!"

"There's no choice," Gale added.

Booker stared hard at Rip.

"Booker, years ago you, Larsen, and I sat around a table and talked about what we might find. Maybe you had a dream it would be like this, but Larsen and I just wanted to prove the Cosega Theory – that humans had lived in some form of an advanced society significantly predating our current timelines." Rip paused, collecting his thoughts. "We found so much more than the Cosega Theory. We found the Cosegans. And what Gale and I began as a quest to unlock the secrets of the strange and wondrous artifact called the Eysen has now turned into an urgent mission to save the world from itself. How can we stop the final Divinations? Is it even possible? Only Clastier can tell us."

"What do you need?" Booker asked.

"A van, a copier, and as many AX agents as we can fit," Gale said.

"Can't we fly you there?" Booker said.

"Don't you think that will attract too much attention?" Rip asked.

"I guess so, in this climate. I'll have a unit on standby to extract you. Get them X34 phones," Booker said to his assistant. "They are scrambled, blocked, blind, and linked to communicate only with other X34s."

As they were leaving, Booker ran up to the van. "Rip, don't you think I should keep the Eysen for safe keeping?"

"I've managed this far," Rip answered. "I'm sure you'll keep us well protected." He patted the backpack that Booker had given him that contained a tracking device they had mutually agreed to be a good precaution.

"Yes. I'll be watching," Booker said. "Good luck. See you in the sun." Booker ran to the helicopter, its rotors spinning.

67

The van pulled up to Teresa's house. Gale and Rip jumped out and ran to the front door. They were afraid she'd been killed and the papers taken.

Gale almost cried when the porch light came on. Teresa opened the door with a surprised look.

"Thank God you're all right," Rip said.

"I could say the same for you Mr. Ripley. The newswoman on TV said you were dead."

Rip couldn't help himself. He hugged her.

"Mind my hip Mr. Ripley, it's been acting up since the rain."

"Teresa, I'm afraid we're in a little bit of a hurry."

"Aren't you always?"

"We need to make another set of copies of the letters and papers."

"Why? Did you lose yours?" She shook her head. "I'm not letting them out of my house again."

"We thought you might say that," Gale said. Rip nodded to Kruse. He carried in a copy machine from the van. "We can do it right in your living room, if you don't mind."

"Well, look at that," Teresa said. "You folks are clever. Sure, come on in. I'll put on some tea. You know, I've read all his papers since you were last here, and it's no wonder those Church leaders in Rome didn't like him."

They followed Teresa inside and Kruse set up the copier before he was dismissed by Teresa. "I'm sure Mr. Ripley can handle some stacks of paper," she said. "You can sweep my front walk if you need something to do," she said while pointing Kruse to the front door. Rip was going to remind her it was dark out, but let it go.

It didn't take long since they were copying copies and not the originals. Rip just had to refill the auto feeder five or six times and they were set.

"I'm sorry, but we have to go," Rip said.

"But you didn't finish your tea," Teresa said.

"There are some bad people after us," Gale explained while Rip gulped his tea. "They may come here and try to hurt you. We can send you somewhere for a while."

"To hide?" she asked, annoyed.

"Think of it as a vacation," Rip said.

"I'm way too old for a vacation," Teresa said. "And have you forgotten? This is Flora's home. Clastier lived here. This place holds too many secrets for me to just up and leave it."

Rip looked at Gale. She shrugged. "You'll be okay?" Rip asked.

"I'm the last protector," Teresa said.

Ninety minutes later, one of Booker's presidential-type helicopters picked them up in Albuquerque to avoid suspicion. From there, against Booker's wishes, they flew to Canyon de Chelly. The Navajo reservation was as far off the grid as one could get and still be within the continental United States. Booker knew the NSA would have a harder time locating them there, but he still wanted to stick to the original plan and get Gale, Rip, and the Eysen out of the country to one of his many offshore hideaways. Rip told him that they would need just a few hours there and could leave in the morning.

During the fifty-minute flight, Gale described the horrible scene at the church in Las Trampas where Larsen was killed.

"Father Jak saved me because he knew what I was doing there. Somehow, Clastier was able to get his message across the decades through probably eight or nine priests. Even though they were Catholic, they preserved letters that went against their Church." Gale's eyes widened. "And do you know why? Because they believed Clastier was right."

"Then what happened to the missing letters?" Rip asked, resisting the urge to kiss her. The impulse both surprised him and seemed natural.

"Maybe they were too controversial about the Church," she said. "But that's just it. They still *believed* it."

"Then why continue in their ministries?"

"Maybe they tucked his message into their sermons. Maybe they knew it wasn't time."

"So where are the letters?"

"Still in that safe," Gale said.

"No." Rip looked at her sternly. "We are *not* going back. Anyway, you know they've been cleaned out by now."

"I know," Gale said. "I just wish we'd beaten Barbeau to San Cristobal."

"We have enough."

"Then let's not risk going to Canyon de Chelly."

"I need to talk to the shaman," Rip said.

"Because of what Booker said about your destiny?"

"Yes," he said. "There's something haunting me about all this."

"The Conway part?"

"That, and the Divinations. That shaman knows something. I don't know what, but I ended the conversation too soon."

Gale just stared at him, smiling.

"What?" he asked, feeling self-conscious.

"You don't sound like such a hardcore scientist anymore," she said. "You've experienced synchronicity, meeting people you were meant to meet and winding up in places where you were meant to be. You believe you lived a life as Conway, and that Clastier knew how to communicate through time." She paused. "The Eysen gave you all that. It changed you."

He nodded. "That's why I have to see the shaman. I still don't understand all of that, and if I'm going to decode the Cosega Sequence I need to know what all of this means. What is the Eysen? Why did I find it?"

68

Jaeger threw his jump rope at a subordinate. "What do you mean they *aren't* there? You found Booker's compound in Taos . . . *empty*!?"

"We didn't locate it in time," the man said.

"Obviously," Jaeger said, appalled. "There must be impressions. They didn't escape in a tunnel, did they?" He yelled across the room, "Find something. Track back, give me everything!"

The technicians were programming computers to review all area satellite data. It would show them any flights in or out of the area by any type of craft. Road traffic was nearly impossible to trace, especially at night. There was just too much of it. But Jaeger drew a circle around Taos.

"Follow everything that has moved inside of this for the past five hours."

"That will take forever," the man said.

"Then you better get started." Jaeger began doing laps. *Where would they go?* he asked himself. "Find out where Barbeau is and check on the Vatican agents, then get the cardinal on the phone." He ran to the monitors. "Where the hell are you weasels?"

The *Exsequor et Protector Ecclesiae* was in the middle of his own crisis when the NSA called. It wasn't a good time to talk, but there would never be a good time.

"Tell me Cardinal," Jaeger began. "Where do you think they are?"

The cardinal was discouraged. If the NSA didn't know where they were, his troubles had just increased infinitely. "Isn't that *your* job?" he asked bitterly.

"Yes, it is my job to use data to find Gaines. It is yours to use knowledge to anticipate where he will go."

"If I were Gaines, I would flee the country."

"Would you? Aren't there pieces to this cursed religious puzzle that he still needs? What happened in San Crisobal? Your man Nanski dead. Gale Asher. Would he go back there? The Pueblo? Chimayó? Some new sacred site that only you people know exists?"

"You listen to me, little man. God almighty may have forsaken his one true Church, and you are playing a game of cat and mouse – a *game*! You think you have power? You think you even know what power is? You read a report that your own department created about what would happen to the world without the Church, and it scared you into making a deal with us." The cardinal struggled to keep from smashing his phone. "Let me tell you what apparently you don't realize. You won't just have a mess to clean up if we crumble, you will fall with us. Catholicism is the pillar of Christianity, a faith your nation was founded on and is, like it or not, the force that still controls your government."

"Are you done Cardinal? With the lecture, I mean," Jaeger said, "because I don't want the Church to fall anymore than you do. We don't have to agree on the reasons or even the methods to prevent it, but I need to know where Gaines might have gone. The Vatican is a trove of secrets and intelligence, and it's woven through this case. Don't you get it? You are helping to bring about your own destruction. Open the damned vaults and let me help you."

The cardinal could not tell him that the vaults had already been opened. That during the last few days, much of the Vatican's treasures and priceless archives had been crated and moved to secret locations around the globe. The plan had been in place for decades, modified and reviewed as recently as a few months earlier. The steps they never hoped to take, and even now the Pope clung to hope, as he stayed secluded, praying that they could still save their religion. But they had to be prepared if they failed to secure the *Ater Dies*. The most important accoutrements of the Church needed to be saved for the day when it could rise again.

"If I were Gaines, I would seek a member of the clergy," the cardinal said.

"You aren't serious?"

"The complex issues that Clastier raises, prophecies, reincarnation, healings, et cetera, and the god-like power of the *Ater Dies*, are too much for a scientist to comprehend and reconcile. He needs a person of faith to show him the way through. God is many things to many people. He wears different faces and is known by various names, but there is more in the universe that we cannot explain, than there is known."

"Gaines is not going to a priest."

"I agree that it's doubtful," the cardinal said impatiently. "For someone like him it may be a Unity minister, a faith healer, a shaman, or even his father."

Suddenly, Jaeger knew exactly where Gaines had gone, and so did the cardinal.

69

Barbeau was parked on a narrow, seldom-used dirt road, leading to Taos Pueblo. He'd been on his way to see the old shopkeeper who had accused Gaines of being Conway. His hope was that the crazy man could shed some light on Clastier. Barbeau had come to the conclusion that Clastier was the key to the entire case. Why else would Gaines and Asher repeatedly risk their lives and the Eysen to trace the life of the nineteenth century priest?

He'd pulled over to take the call. It was from someone he never expected to hear from, even as crazy as things had become, and it turned out to be the most disturbing call of his life. Once the call was over, he pulled out his revolver and fired into the windshield. An explosion of shattered chunks of glass covered the hood of the car. Enough of it had flown into the car that a pile fell from his lap as he got out and stood. He didn't notice his face and arm were bleeding. All he wanted was a church to burn or a priest to blame, but he was alone, and there was no one to blame but himself.

After all these years his daughter had called, not to say she loved him or forgave him. She needed help. His only grandson, a seven year-old boy, was attending a Catholic school, not for religious reasons, but because it was the best private school they could afford in Los Angeles. A priest at the school had molested him.

"They aren't going to do anything about it Daddy," she cried. "That monster is just getting transferred to another school. You're the FBI. You have to arrest him or something!"

He couldn't shake the sound of his daughter's destroyed voice, the helplessness of her son's stolen innocence. His daughter and his grandson had suffered something beyond crime, more proof that hell only exists on earth, growing like poison in paradise.

Finally, his badge, which had cost him his family, could be used to help. But even as he thought that, he had the realization that it was too late. Vengeance might be obtained, but the damage was indelible. If there wasn't enough evidence to arrest and convict the priest, he would kill him. Even if they could get a conviction, Barbeau wanted to kill the priest, slowly, over several days.

Then it hit him. He had, in his possession, the means to destroy the entire Catholic Church. Not just one priest, but *all* of them.

⬤

Barbeau had figured out where Gaines was going by good old-fashioned detective work. A pair of agents had been staking out Teresa's house ever since the massacre in Las Trampas. When they reported that Gaines and Asher had shown up, Barbeau ordered them to follow at a safe distance. By the time Gale and Rip made it to Albuquerque and boarded Booker's helicopter, Barbeau was in the air himself. The Bureau tracked their flight on radar. Barbeau and two agents landed not long after Gale and Rip, but Barbeau hadn't wanted to risk detection. They set down in a remote section where they had a couple of Jeeps waiting.

The plan was to drive in at first light. More agents were watching the rim with night vision. They had a pretty good idea of the section in which Gaines was hiding. The DIRT agents would cover the west side, and the Barbeau would take the east. He set it up that way because he wanted to talk to Gaines alone.

Barbeau didn't sleep much. Under normal circumstances he didn't like tents, but after the call from his daughter he felt trapped, and spent much of the night in front of the fire. It was only the thought of killing the priest who had hurt his grandson and seeing the Church fall that kept him sane until morning.

The NSA and the cardinal didn't tell each other, but they had both reached the same conclusion. Sean Stradler had reported the earlier meeting with the shaman. It was part of the file that had been shared with the Vatican. Jaeger liked it. Gaines needed a remote spot with trusted friends and a "great" spiritual adviser to sort out everything. He ran grids on the area, and by late night they had traced the flight. At dawn, the sky over Canyon de Chelly would be filled with parachuting Special Ops.

The cardinal had already sent Vatican agents to the Canyon. There were only two of them close enough, but they got there ahead of Barbeau and the NSA. The cardinal wanted Gaines alive, but if any other government or agency had a chance at getting him first, they were to kill him. "Bring me the *Ater Dies*," the cardinal had said. "That is all that matters."

70

Rip's old friends from the Navajo Nation, Tahoma and Mai, were waiting with horses and flashlights, having been notified by Booker to expect Gale, Rip, and Kruse. The helicopter had landed on the canyon floor so the ride would not be long. As a precaution, the pilot moved it back to the nearby town of Shiprock. Several other AX agents loitered nearby. Only Kruse would ride with them.

Tahoma greeted Gale, who introduced him to Kruse. They talked briefly about their last visit, when Tahoma had rescued her. She didn't have great memories of the place. It reminded her of Sean's betrayal and death, and the beginning of the split with Rip. Only the encounter with Sani-Niyol, the shaman, had been good.

Mai hugged Rip tightly and whispered into his ear. "Kiss me like one of us is about to go away forever and I'll pretend to forget the past."

"I am an archaeologist," he replied. "I live in the past."

"And we left our chance back there?" she said, looking over at Gale.

"I'm learning that the past is more a part of the present than the moment we are actually in."

"And what part does the past play in the future?" she asked playfully.

"That's what I'm here to discover," Rip said as Gale came over. He helped her up onto her horse. Rip recalled his last nighttime ride. He'd known so little then.

Tahoma rode up next to Rip. "Old friend."

"Forgive me for putting you at risk once again," Rip said. "We'll be gone with the sun."

"Stay for a thousand suns, brother."

They found Sani-Niyol meditating in front of a small campfire. Only after they had quietly sat around the fire did he look up, smiling. Tahoma asked the old shaman permission to add more wood. "Yes, please. So many to keep warm," he said. "I'm glad you've returned."

"Thank you," Rip said sitting next to him. "I was hoping you could help me understand a few things . . . about the past."

"The past is always singing. We just ignore the music."

Rip nodded knowingly. "When we last spoke, you mentioned a man named Conway. As I understand it, he spent his lifetime trying to suppress the very thing I am trying to preserve, and yet you claim he and I were the same."

"Karma brought you here. She is not so difficult to understand once you realize that Karma never forgets, but it is not a grudge she is holding. It is your hand as she lovingly guides you back to the light."

Rip thought about that for a moment. "So, if I had not lived a bad life, I wouldn't be here trying to repair it now."

"One cannot recognize the light until he has lived in darkness," Sani-Niyol said.

"May we ask a specific question?" Gale asked.

The shaman nodded, smiling.

"We have an extremely old object that we don't completely understand. We need to know how to find its answers."

"It's not within the object, it's within you," he said, pointing to Rip. "The answers come from many places."

Rip wanted to say that Gale had asked a specific question and the shaman had given what he considered to be a vague answer, but he held his tongue.

"When we look into the past," Sani-Niyol began, "in our arrogance, we believe we know more than the ancestors knew." He nodded and pointed at Rip. "If you want to learn from the past, you must see with the eyes of the ancestors . . . not through the lens of a scientist."

Gale, sensing Rip's feeling of contempt at being told how to view the past, placed her hand on his wrist. The action stopped him from pointing out that he was considered one of the foremost experts in the world at learning from the past.

"It must be done differently," Sani-Niyol said. "There is often more truth in dreams than in the waking world."

"I'm not sure I understand," Rip replied.

San-Niyol smiled. "Of course you don't understand, you have only just been told. As long as you have heard what I said, it will happen. There are three steps to learning: seeing or hearing, experience, and time. You have taken the first step, and sometimes journeys are very long."

"I don't have that much time," Rip said.

"That is all." The shaman waved his hand. Mai tapped Rip, who wasn't ready to leave. They thanked Sani-Niyol and rode back to their former campsite. Rip felt frustrated that he didn't get the answers he had hoped.

There was already a tent set up and wood for a morning fire. Mai and Tahoma said goodnight.

"I'll see you in the morning," Rip said to Mai.

"I don't think so," she said. "I prefer to remember the stars as they were on the first night we loved."

Rip hugged her long and then said farewell with his eyes as they shared a last, teary glance.

Although they were both exhausted, Gale and Rip stayed up watching the Eysen and talking until almost three a.m. The light filled the tent as Gale saw, for the first time, the three-hundred-sixty-degree projection capabilities of the ancient artifact. Rip could only kneel in the small tent, but he began moving the images to reveal more details.

They reached a place where he'd long wanted to go; inside a Cosegan city. Huge shiny domes and spheres dominated the skyline. Giant, doughnut-shaped buildings, some lying flat, others standing on end, were all set in a lush landscape. There were skyscrapers much larger than anything in the modern world. The circular towers, capped with giant spheres, were surrounded by expansive rings, giving them a Saturn-like appearance. Others structures, stacked in the distance in clusters, looked like massive bunches of silver grapes.

Rip zoomed in and they were able to enter one of the great buildings. The interior was the size of a football stadium, and it was filled with holographic circles and dashes. "It's the Cosega Sequence!" Rip exclaimed.

The Crying Man stepped out from a corridor and welcomed them with a bow. Gale could hardly breathe. As Crying Man moved through the building, the Cosega Sequences scattered like autumn leaves in the wind. When the symbols reassembled in his wake, the space around filled with the rest of the Sequence – spinning Earth, trees, oceans, stars, and the flashing pulses of light.

"What is the Sequence?" Rip asked.

Crying Man cupped his hands like he was holding an invisible ball, and then moved his arms above his head and opened them. A glowing orb floated out from them.

Gale gasped.

He stared at them for a long time as the orb floated between them. Rip tried to pick up on the telepathic communication, but it didn't happen.

"Are you getting anything?" he asked Gale. "Their language is circular, using telepathy to go around."

"Mind to eyes to eyes to mind," Gale said.

"Yes."

"He's saying the Sequence is about everything. It has all been shown to you."

"Maybe I'm not smart enough," Rip said.

"No, it's like Sani-Niyol said, the three parts of learning. You've seen it, now you just need the experience and time to kick in."

"Time?" Rip said. "Do you think we have a lot of time?"

"I think he said that there are two questions with the same answer."

"Where's he going?" Rip asked.

As Crying Man left the building, he turned, shook his head, and the Eysen went dark.

Monday July 24th

The vibrating buzz of the X34 phone startled Rip awake. He crawled out of his sleeping bag and left the tent. Gale hardly stirred.

"Senator Monroe is dead," Booker said.

"How?"

"Assassinated. The initial intel chatter says it was the Mossad."

"Wow. But he didn't even have the Eysen."

"Apparently our theory was wrong. The prospect of a Monroe Presidency already made the Israelis nervous. The fact that he might also possess an Eysen was too much to take. They obviously have a mole inside the NSA or the Vatican."

"Probably the two most secure entities on Earth. How could they?"

"Don't underestimate the Mossad, but there is no other way they could know that the NSA and the Vatican have a pact to share the Eysen in order to keep the Catholic Church alive, and the neutral party that would keep the Eysen was Monroe."

"Incredible. Either way, we may be better off without him in the White House, but the thought of being unable to avoid the other Divinations is sobering."

"Terrifying."

"I think I have an idea about the Cosega Sequence. I need to do one more thing. I think we'll be ready to leave here in a couple of hours."

"I want you out *now*."

"I need an hour."

"BLAX is on standby to pull you out."

Only Rip's complete exhaustion had allowed him to sleep. He'd been upset by the disappearance of the Crying Man, feeling as if there was never enough time with the Eysen to understand it, but in the night he'd remembered something Sani-Niyol had said.

The information inside the Eysen was too much to take in all at once. Those three steps of learning were the key. Time; Clastier had had forty years to study the Eysen, and he didn't even write about what it was or explain the Sequence. He had used it to glean the Attestations and Divinations, but Rip's purpose was different. He needed to know what the Sequence was, and that had overshadowed Rip's first question as an archaeologist. What *is* the Eysen?

The two questions that the Crying Man had referred to: What is the Sequence? What is the Eysen? They were two questions with one answer. If he could find that answer, would he be able to stop the Divinations? He knew what to ask Sani-Niyol now. Are the past and the future the same thing? When he saw the Cosegan city up close, far more advanced than any futurist had ever dreamed, he had to wonder. Is time a circle? He scribbled a note for Gale and then left to find the shaman.

"Gaines!" Barbeau yelled.

Rip froze, but he knew the voice. Slowly, he turned and faced Dixon Barbeau. Surprisingly there was no gun pointed at him. The FBI agent was only holding a book.

"I've got something for you," Barbeau said.

Rip, trying to catch his breath, looked around for the ambush.

"Another lucky day for you Gaines. Because I'm not going to arrest you today either," Barbeau said. "There are enough FBI and NSA agents around here to do that. But if you do get away, I want you to have this." Barbeau handed him the evidence bag.

Rip still didn't speak.

"Inside you'll find a book about Clastier that I picked up in San Cristobal, as well as a translation."

"Why?" Rip asked, unsure how he'd made such a friend in the FBI agent who'd been tracking him for weeks.

"It's nothing personal Gaines. Let's just say I'm doing it for the greater good."

Rip was about to say something, but a bullet cut through him and he fell to the ground.

Barbeau pulled his weapon and ducked, but before he could find cover or the source of the shot, he got hit. As he fell, his gun landed inches from Gaines.

Seconds later, two Vatican agents, a man and woman, emerged from the scrub.

"Kill the other one, but we're supposed to try to keep Gaines alive," the woman said.

Just as the agent was about to shoot Barbeau, Rip got the gun and fired at the man. Miraculously, the shot hit his neck, and the agent folded over and collapsed. The female agent yelled, "Drop it, Gaines, or I'll shoot!"

Before Gaines could decide what to do, Kruse shot the other agent in the head. "Number five," he whispered to himself.

Gale had been on her way to meet Rip at Sani-Niyol's. She

heard the shots and ran to Gaines. "It's my side or my thigh," he said. "I don't know, too much blood."

Barbeau rolled over. "Thanks, Gaines," he moaned.

Kruse pivoted and trained his weapon on Barbeau.

"No!" Gaines shouted. "Don't shoot!"

Kruse kept his weapon aimed, but turned to Rip.

"He's on our side," Rip said.

"I guess I am," Barbeau said, thinking it for the first time. "My enemy's enemy is my friend."

Eight minutes later, one of Booker's presidential-type helicopters landed, and suddenly Gale and Rip were airborne. Kruse stayed behind. He had a plan. After getting quick approval from Booker via an X34 phone, he made preparations while waiting for a BLAX unit of mercenaries to arrive. Kruse talked to Barbeau while giving him first aid. It would help if he lived.

As the BLAX team landed in their military helicopter, the sky above filled with NSA paratroopers. "This is insane," the BLAX commander said to Kruse.

"I know, but we can do this. We have to end it."

The mercenaries loaded the bodies of the Vatican agents onto the chopper and the BLAX pilot readied to lift off. Then, at the last moment, he bailed. Barbeau was still too close to the helicopter and could be injured, but they had to risk it. As Kruse and the BLAX agents retreated into the canyon, they fired a shoulder-mounted missile at their own chopper. The explosion was far greater than would have been normal due to a fifty-five-gallon drum of fuel already on board with the dead Vatican agents.

DIRT agents reached Barbeau a few minutes later and called in an air-ambulance. A fiery plume had blown over him. Most of the burns were minor, but the pain helped him act convincingly when the first NSA Special Ops commandos showed up a couple of minutes later. Once they IDed him, they asked him the whereabouts of Gaines and Asher.

"They shot me as they got on that chopper," Barbeau said, as he winced in pain.

"Who?" one of the Special Ops soldiers asked.

"Gaines and Asher," Barbeau said, as though it should be obvious.

"The suspects are in *that?*" another soldier asked, pointing to the intense fire and shielding his face.

"Yes," Barbeau said. "That's not one of our choppers! Now, can someone get me out of here? It's a little hot."

"EMTs will be here any minute," a DIRT agent interjected.

"Who blew it up?" the first NSA commando asked.

"I don't know," Barbeau said.

A classified theory quickly emerged that the Eysen had caused the explosion to be larger and more intense than normal because of the extraordinary materials that must have been used to make the artifact.

Later the attack would be blamed on the Mossad. The only one who didn't buy it was Jaeger, but the pressure proved too much for him. Within hours of Monroe's assassination and the purported death of Gaines and Asher, Jaeger suffered a massive heart attack while jogging outside the command center. His superiors suspected the Vatican, Booker, or the Mossad might have caused his death to appear natural, but his wife refused to allow an autopsy on religious grounds. They were Jewish.

72

On Booker's spacious helicopter, a medic tended to Rip's wound. He was very lucky the bullet went through his upper thigh. It didn't hit anything vital, and had made a clean exit. Rip read the translated copy of the San Cristobal journal while Gale read the original. A devout follower of Clastier had written it.

An entirely new section of Clastier's work was contained in the pages called Inspirations, which were short quotations taken from his many sermons, such as "Judgment, anger, hatred, and jealously are some of the poisons of fear; why would you allow this venom in your heart?" But it wasn't the Inspirations that excited them most.

Buried near the back of the book was a new Divination. Even though the Empty Man one, about Monroe's assassination, had already come to pass, they called this new one "the sixth final Divination." It described a utopia after a great plague. Clastier himself was confused whether it was 2065 or 2115, but in either case it was a wonderful world.

Humankind had completely quit fossil fuels, instead solar and wind powered everything. It had been decades since war of any kind, and even illness had been all but been eradicated. Hunger did not exist, as food was abundant. Space exploration was the leading industry. However, the most startling aspect of this future that Clastier had described more than a hundred and fifty years ago was that the Earth's population was nearly three billion, a figure that might have seemed staggeringly large to Clastier, when in his time the total number of people barely topped one billion.

"But we have more than seven billion people. What happens to four billion people in the next fifty to a hundred years?" Gale asked weakly.

"There is only one answer," Rip said. "In order to reach the glory of the sixth Divination, we must go through the horror of the others."

Gale opened her journal. "Monroe is dead. Next the Catholic Church falls. Then the global pandemics and super-viruses wipe out vast numbers. After that, climate destabilization." Gale looked at Rip, unable to read the last one. The devastation in her eyes pained him.

"And then World War III, or something like it," Rip said. "You wouldn't think we'd have much fight left in us."

"Humans always seem to be ready for a fight, but we have to find a way to stop his prophecies," she said.

"If we do, we might miss the utopia," Rip said.

"So!?" Gale demanded, visibly shaken. "If we don't, four billion people are going to miss it anyway!"

He took her hand. "Don't worry, we'll try."

"Professor," one of the BLAX agents interrupted. "We'll be landing soon. The rest of your journey will be by boat." Booker wanted them well off the radar, and had arranged one of his luxury yachts to take them to a private island off the coast of Mexico.

●

Once on the yacht, Gale and Rip settled into a spacious cabin and took out the Eysen. The Sequence projected across the room, and soon they were back in the Cosegan city. Rip's leg wouldn't allow him to stand, but he was still able to direct the action from his bed. They went into some kind of science hall filled with stars, planets, volcanoes, and churning oceans, all life-like. The technology was beyond imagination. Every detail could be split and analyzed down to the subatomic level. It reminded them of Booker's Universal Quantum Physics project because everything contained a glowing energy. It was the one unifying element among each thing they encountered. Rip told Gale that when he'd first seen a projection appear outside of the Eysen, it was of himself.

"The miniature version of me peeled layers of myself away, just like we're doing with these objects, and the same light-energy was inside me too."

The hall of science was so big that soon they realized it kept expanding as they went in further. Soon, people and animals were there. Gale could easily break them down into layers, and always found the same light-energy. Whenever they tried to go beyond the light energy, it just got smaller, but otherwise did not change.

"I finally get it," Rip whispered, getting painfully to his feet.

73

Gale moved until she was in front of him. "What?" she asked.

Rip limped around the cabin, eyes darting wildly, arms moving to switch the scene.

"Tell me," Gale demanded.

"Don't you see?" Rip said breathlessly. "It's the big bang."

"How—"

"It's where we came from. That's the end of the Cosega Sequence!" Rip pointed to the projected images. "Look." He brought up the Sequence, then stood in the middle and separated the circles and dashes until the same central point of light emerged. "The Cosegans are saying the same thing that Clastier wrote, 'We're all part of the whole.' But they're showing us." He moved his hands in circular motions. "The big bang wasn't just the beginning of our universe, it was the beginning of *us*. We started as that point of light. Call it the God point."

"God?" Gale asked.

"For lack of a better word," Rip said, the irony not lost on him. They'd just exposed one religion, he certainly didn't want to create another. "God, the universe, great spirit, collective consciousness, whatever you'd like to call it, but for this conversation I want to draw a distinction between the matter and the spiritual."

"All of it really being energy," Gale said. "The same energy."

"Exactly. That's what I'm saying, what Clastier said, and what the Cosegans are showing us." Rip moved his hands again, causing the projection to swirl. "Look, the big bang wasn't just *matter* flying apart, it was *us* flying apart. The moment the universe formed in that violent explosion, we, as God, as Spirit, also exploded. And, like the universe, we continue to expand and move apart. We continue to shift and be in motion as we get farther away from God, us, each other . . . ourselves."

"A shift in consciousness as we expand with the stars."

"Yes! That's what the Cosega Sequence is . . . more than the history of the universe, it is a demonstration of who, or rather what, we are." Rip stared deeply into her eyes. "We're pieces of light flying through the darkness. Apart we are diminished, together we are everything."

Gale and Rip remained silent for a moment.

"Then it begs the question, was the big bang some kind of colossal cosmic accident?" Gale finally asked. "Maybe 'one with the universe' isn't just a slogan. Maybe we should all be trying to get back together. Maybe that is the one way to find the truth about God."

"Who knows?" He looked down at the Eysen. "I wonder if the Cosegans even figured out that answer. We have to keep looking, and now that the Sequence is unlocked, we can get inside and find all the answers."

"And maybe stop the Divinations," Gale said.

"I hope so," Rip added. "They left it for us. We were meant to find it for a reason."

The cabin went dark. For a moment, as they stood in such darkness, they believed they were dead. The Eysen had sucked all light from the room, and then suddenly, a burst of light exploded so brightly that they fell to the ground, covering their eyes.

The big bang progressed through the formation of the galaxies and individual planets. It took only fifteen or twenty minutes for them to see billions of years race by and eventually reach the part of the Sequence with which they were most familiar, the spinning Earth, shifting, tectonic plates. Then, it continued past what they had seen until billions of points of light covered the planet. The lights became people. The Sequence was complete. The overlaid circles and dashes – the language of the Cosegans – told the story of all creation, who we are, and where we came from.

They stood wearily, drained from the spectacle. Rip reached out to steady himself on Gale. Under the stars, on top of the world, floating toward freedom, Rip kissed Gale, and they held each other with the passion of prisoners freed. When they finally let go, in her eyes he saw a fleeting glimpse of all he'd seen in the Eysen, all that ever was.

"Oh my God," Gale said, looking at the images racing by behind Rip.

He turned and almost fell backwards. Every event of both of their lives played like a silent movie behind them, and then he saw Conway, and other lifetimes. In some Gale and Rip were together. It went on and on.

"Do you realize what this is?" Gale asked without waiting for him to answer. "The Eysen holds the Akashic Records."

"What?"

"Akasha is an ancient word meaning sky. Many people believe that all the accumulated knowledge and experience that has ever occurred, or ever will, exists in the ethereal. It's called the Akashic Records."

"I've heard of it, but it's a New Age myth," Rip said.

"Is it?" Gale pointed to the images moving all around them. "You said yourself, 'The Eysen knows everything. Not just about Earth, but the entire universe, even the future.' That's the Akashic Records. I can't believe I didn't put it together before this."

"Then the Eysen isn't just a computer," Rip said, unable to deny the obvious proof before him. "The Cosegans somehow managed to manufacture an instrument to view eternity."

"There is no way to comprehend the power we now possess."

EPILOGUE

A year later Booker's company began selling a consumer version of the Eysen, a computer so advanced that it couldn't even be called a computer. It created a new category known as Information Navigation Units, or INUs. Within the first eighteen months, more than 450 million Eysens were sold. It was the most successful product launch in history. Total sales were expected to reach a billion units in the next year.

The consumer version, identical in appearance to the one Rip pulled from the Virginia cliff, made it impossible for those who didn't believe the original blew up with Gaines and Asher to find the real one. The NSA kept the file open, but no progress had been made since Jaeger's death.

The Vatican first tried to deny the validity of the information contained in the commercially released Eysens, but once the consumer version came preloaded with the Akashic app and everyone was able to access the truth, Clastier's Divination about the end of the Catholic Church proved to be as accurate as all of his other prophesies. Rome fell quickly.

It wasn't just the proof of human origin that buried the Church. The clarity and meaning portrayed in the Eysens showed how the weight of religious trappings had held the world back. With the spotlight on the Vatican, one issue after another erupted: major financial scandals, widening sex abuse, the existence of the Vatican Secret Service.

Then an anonymous organization leaked millions of pages of documents over the Internet. They detailed Church atrocities dating back centuries, and specifically highlighted World War II through the present day. Investigations were launched, resulting in a stunning, and previously unthinkable event when the remaining Vatican archives were raided by a joint committee of twelve nations and Church assets were seized around the globe.

Booker worked tirelessly to recover some of the hidden Vatican treasures and archives, with little luck. For years, Church leaders had been preparing for the end, and they'd had weeks to implement their final plans. He was able to intercept the "Asheville" casing that Vatican agents had taken, along with the original Clastier Papers, and he turned it over to the scientific community for study. Many disputed the age, claiming Gaines had brought it to Virginia from a much more recent site in South America, but plenty of others sided with him.

Behind the scenes, Booker was also instrumental in navigating the many legal obstacles involved in testing the U.S. Forest Service site where Rip had found the Eysen. With new testing equipment, the cliff had been conclusively dated to be 10.8 million years old, but even with the latest techniques available, the exact age of the casing could not be determined.

Attorney General Dover resigned, and the FBI Director was appointed to replace him. Special Agent Dixon Barbeau recovered from his wounds, quit the Bureau, and became a freelance investigator for a single client: DIRT. He was successful in bringing charges that resulted in the prosecution of the priest who molested his grandson. Barbeau had also begun reconciling with his daughter.

Booker himself had too much influence to be arrested, but the threat of assassination followed him, and he rarely stayed anywhere for more than a few days at a time. His mystery and wealth continued to grow.

"Taking a page from the NSA's playbook and faking our deaths was what saved us, but it's not without a price," Rip said to Gale.

"I know. But Booker thinks that by next spring it may be safe to meet my parents. He'll have someone contact them and arrange for a vacation in Mexico. Then he'll have BLAX sneak them out of the country and I can see them briefly in Cuba. Grinley's still living there, you know?"

"That'll be quite a shock for your parents to learn you're actually alive."

She looked over at Kruse and Harmer. They'd become good friends, as the agents were always there, on guard, and acting as a conduit for all the intel AX collected. The island was beautiful. They had all they needed, but sometimes it was small. They hoped it would only be for a couple more years.

The explorations into the Eysen were never-ending. Rip had discovered two other civilizations that had risen and vanished long before "modern" humans appeared. It was overwhelming to be able to see and know everything, something the consumer Eysens couldn't do yet, but Booker was promising regular upgrades. The world was hungry for Eysen 2.0.

Gale had spent months working on the Clastier Papers, editing the originals, as well as missing pages that had surfaced, including the Inspirations, and even excerpting some of his letters to Flora and her notes about the ones to Padre Romero. Soon they would be ready for release. For now, she was planning to leave out the remaining Divinations, including the sixth one. They were still looking for ways to stop, or at least change them. "The only hope for the future," Rip said many times, "is locked in the past." But time was ticking away.

After the void created by Catholicism's collapse, along with other mystical events seemingly brought about by people's exposure to the Eysens and Booker's Universal Quantum Physics research, a languishing group called the Inner Movement had suddenly grown more popular. Booker disagreed with Rip on one major point saying, "The only hope for the future is locked within each of us."

END OF BOOK THREE
Seven years after they "died" the hunt resumes – discover COSEGA SPHERE (book four of the Cosega Sequence) available now at your favorite store

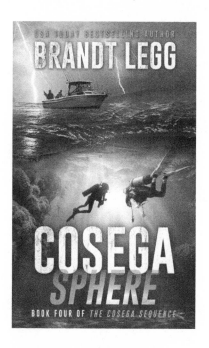

**He found proof of the impossible,
Now . . . he must do the impossible.**

Seven years after their "deaths," Gale and Rip have just three days to find the Cosegans inside the Eysen-Sphere, solve the five

Cosega mysteries, stop the final Divinations, and save their daughter. Three days with everyone after them, three days to unlock the past, survive the present, and change the future. There is not enough time. It is truly impossible. But then time is a funny thing.

Dictate enough of the past . . . you may just dominate the future.

COSEGA SPHERE (book four of the Cosega Sequence) available now.

A NOTE FROM THE AUTHOR

- *Thanks for sharing the adventure!*
- **Please help** - If you enjoyed it, please post a review wherever you got the book. (even a few words). Reviews are the greatest way to help an author. And, please tell your friends.
- **I'd love to hear from you** – really. Questions, comments, whatever. Email me through my website. I'll definitely respond (within a few days).
- **Join my Inner Circle** - If you want to be the first to hear about my new releases, advance reads, occasional news and more, visit BrandtLegg.com

ABOUT THE AUTHOR

USA TODAY Bestselling Author Brandt Legg uses his unusual real life experiences to create page-turning novels. He's traveled with CIA agents, dined with senators and congressmen, mingled with astronauts, chatted with governors and presidential candidates, had a private conversation with a Secretary of Defense he still doesn't like to talk about, hung out with Oscar and Grammy winners, had drinks at the State Department, been pursued by tabloid reporters, and spent a birthday at the White House by invitation from the President of the United States.

At age eight, Legg's father died suddenly, plunging his family into poverty. Two years later, while suffering from crippling migraines, he started in business, and turned a hobby into a multi-million-dollar empire. National media dubbed him the "Teen Tycoon," and by the mid-eighties, Legg was one of the top young entrepreneurs in America, appearing as high as number twenty-four on the list (when Steve Jobs was #1, Bill Gates #4, and Michael Dell #6). Legg still jokes that he should have gone into computers.

By his twenties, after years of buying and selling businesses, leveraging, and risk-taking, the high-flying Legg became ensnarled in the financial whirlwind of the junk bond eighties. The stock market crashed and a firestorm of trouble came down. The Teen Tycoon racked up more than a million dollars in legal fees, was betrayed by those closest to him, lost his entire fortune, and ended up serving time for financial improprieties.

After a year, Legg emerged from federal prison, chastened and wiser, and began anew. More than twenty-five years later, he's now using all that hard-earned firsthand knowledge of conspiracies, corruption and high finance to weave his tales. Legg's books pulse with authenticity.

His series have excited nearly a million readers around the world. Although he refused an offer to make a television movie about his life as a teenage millionaire, his autobiography is in the works. There has also been interest from Hollywood to turn his thrillers into films. With any luck, one day you'll see your favorite characters on screen.

He lives in the Pacific Northwest, with his wife and son, writing full time, in several genres, containing the common themes of adventure, conspiracy, and thrillers. Of all his pursuits, being an author and crafting plots for novels is his favorite.

For more information, please visit his website, or to contact Brandt directly, email him: Brandt@BrandtLegg.com, he loves to hear from readers and always responds!

BrandtLegg.com

BOOKS BY BRANDT LEGG

Chasing Rain

Chasing Fire

Chasing Wind

Chasing Dirt

Chasing Life

Cosega Search (Cosega Sequence #1)

Cosega Storm (Cosega Sequence #2)

Cosega Shift (Cosega Sequence #3)

Cosega Sphere (Cosega Sequence #4)

CapWar ELECTION (CapStone Conspiracy #1)

CapWar EXPERIENCE (CapStone Conspiracy #2)

CapWar EMPIRE (CapStone Conspiracy #3)

The Last Librarian (Justar Journal #1)

The Lost TreeRunner (Justar Journal #2)

The List Keepers (Justar Journal #3)

Outview (Inner Movement #1)

Outin (Inner Movement #2)

Outmove (Inner Movement #3)

ACKNOWLEDGMENTS

This year was a marathon to get these books out. Roanne Legg sacrificed much of her own writing time so that I could make the deadlines. It was a gift that after the difficult first half of 2014, my mother, Barbara Blair, was able to read the Cosega Sequence. Bonnie Brown Koeln, who bent time in order to make it all work. Elizabeth Chumney fought prepositions and commas on my pages even while fighting real life battles. There are others who have so often helped in countless ways at just the "write" time: Mollie Gregory, Mike Sager, Harriet Greene, Martin Goldman, Gene Legg, and especially to all the readers around the world who have taken the time to contact me. And finally to Teakki, who patiently waited, made easier by a beautiful Tiger, until I finished writing each day.